HUNTER'S HARDWARE

DEDICATION

TO MY FAMILY, I WROTE THIS ONE FOR YOU.

BOOK - PG

THIS BOOK REQUIRES PARENTAL GUIDANCE FOR

MODERATE LANGUAGE, ON-PAGE ANIMAL DEATHS,

MENTION OF WEAPONS AND HUNTING TERMS, AND

A CENTRAL ROMANTIC PLOTLINE.

CHAPTER ONE

NASH

This client will change my life. Big ones always do. Slide deck, prepared. Numbers look good. I am ready. Hustling into the bathroom, my fade looks fresh. My barber left the length just right. Suit looks sharp. Face? Handsome as always. I rub the stubble that's grown in since this morning, thanking my father for making me such a distinguished gentleman. Then I'm back into the hall, whistling as I walk.

Time to crush it.

The conference room is like a fishbowl, with windows on every side. Standing at the head of the table, I connect my laptop to the display and prepare the presentation. The sounds of the city sing to my left as the door to my right swings open silently. When I glance up, I see him.

Mr. Jack Collister.

Unlike my partner and the filthy pack of interns who escort him into our luxurious enterprise with offers of still or sparkling water, Jack wears jeans and a pearl-snap button-down. A hat as wide as the luxury light fixtures lining the hall sits atop his head, marking him as the wealthiest cowboy I've ever known. Beside him, his lawyer, Lane Wright, wears a similar getup. I'd call it an outfit, but that wouldn't do it justice. At the very least, Lane threw a tweed sport coat over his ensemble. A half-step to his other side stood Mrs. Collister.

When preparing my presentation, I practiced extra care for her. The women in my office often told me I could make a priest want to cry from my presentations—more boring than sermons. Men in suits, sitting in a boardroom, liked my straightforward approach to data and numbers. Black and white looked sleek, professional. For Mr. and Mrs. Collister, I added color, dimension, and design. I answered questions they might have before they asked them and presented them to make them feel like the smartest person in the room.

My partner smiles, clapping our client on the shoulder as I reach my hand forward to shake.

"Mr. Collister, this is Nash Carter. He is a partner in our firm, and he would be your point of contact if we did business."

Jack shakes my hand, and I meet the firm press of his grip, keeping the connection between us short. The smell of hard work seems to radiate from the man.

"It's a pleasure to meet you, Mr. Collister." His wife giggles lightly, and I give her a kind smile, "And you, Mrs. Collister."

"I've never been treated so formally," she whispers. It's meant for her husband, and he smiles down at her like she's the secret to life's mysteries. His head bends, hat blocking the view of a sweet moment between man and wife.

Husky words whisper, "Get used to it, baby. The suits like it this way." Then, he turns to me and says, "Can't wait to see what you have prepared."

Jack twirls his wife beneath his arm, leading her by the small of her back to the chairs at the back of the room. All the *suits* find their seats as well, and then I begin.

The presentation goes without a flaw. Every point I endeavored to make met a confident reception. They asked all the right questions, and I provided all the planned answers. My partner enhanced my hard work, and by the end, Jack Collister and his account were mine for the taking.

Every man in the room stayed silent while we allowed the client to look through his crisp, bound report. When the thin leather cover closed, I expected a handshake, an acceptance, a 'let's sign those papers.'

Always expect the unexpected.

"Any of y'all hunt? Fish?"

The room couldn't grow any quieter if it tried. All eyes shot to me as I tried to recall a single day on this earth where I desired time spent on such archaic outdoor activities. Humanity worked past a mere need for survival. As people, our capabilities now extend to self-actualization. So, when I could buy my meat at a grocery store, why would I attempt to hunt or gather it myself?

"I grew up hunting grouse with my dad," an intern interjects, earning a glare from my partner. I noted his silence as the client huffed.

"No. Anyone can kill a bird. I meant big game. Deer, elk, bears even."

The room goes silent once again, and I watch all my hard work melt away. It didn't matter that I provided him every comfort a firm like ours could provide. Jack Collister was 'one of those' clients.

Once in a while, 'one of those' clients existed. They were the men made of money who only spent it based on values and morals. They didn't care if you could triple or quadruple their return. If you didn't have dinner with your family once a week or stay faithful to your wife on a Vegas boys' night, you weren't worth their time. They were the antithesis

4

of Wolf on Wall Street men, and more often than not, they hated *suits*. That pearl-snap button-down that screamed money forty-five minutes ago acted as my first hint, and I had ignored it.

Jack clicks his tongue against the roof of his mouth, sighing deeply. "Your numbers look good. I love your company, but I can't trust a man who hasn't killed his own dinner."

Standing with his own team, my partner prepares to walk him out. My heart pounds and the urge to fight sings through my blood. I could be a survivalist, if that's what he needed. Channeling my aggression into a better form, I stand, slamming my palms on the table. All eyes turn to me, and I can see my partner's pinched lips.

His opinions decorate his face. We both know it's stupid to bend to 'one of those' clients, because once you bend once, you'll have to bend again. Then, suddenly, you're twisted into a salty pretzel, begging for the day you took on the account so you could turn it down.

Unfortunately, Jack Collister wasn't just 'one of those' clients; he also held the key to 'one of those' accounts. The ones that fed your family well after you retired and bought your mom diamonds for Christmas.

My mouth worked faster than I did. "Now, wait. If all you need is a man willing to kill for his meat, I can be that guy."

Jack doesn't sit, but he also doesn't exit. He waits. He listens.

"I've never killed for my dinner before, but I'll learn. I have what it takes to be the man you need for this account."

Maintaining eye contact with Jack, my body language begs him to see I'm the real deal. There's a man behind his suit, and it's the guy he needs. He breaks the stare first, glancing down at his wife. My eyes follow his to Mrs. Collister's, and the petite brunette shrugs her shoulders.

"Bring him to camp. See if he can deliver."

Jack's eyes flick to his lawyers, and the man gives him the same nod of approval.

"Call it a trial run. We can write it into your contract, and if he's able to bag a buck, then we'll sign with his firm."

I don't allow my face to betray the churning storm inside me. If the only hoop I had to jump through to sign this deal required me to kill Bambi, I could manage. Weeks and weeks of lawyer negotiations rejected deals, and new proposals were comparatively worse than a single animal death by my hand. Plus, how hard could it be?

My client turned back to me. "Season starts in late August. Our family has a special spot they start camping in around the middle of the month. Meet me in Blacktail Creek first of September, and be prepared to make your first kill."

"Of course, sir. I'll be there."

Our hands came together one last time, and my fate was sealed.

For the next month, my late nights were filled with Hunter's Education courses and long-range shooting lessons. Turns out, killing for your own dinner required a lot more knowledge than point and shoot. I learned about safety and gear, and earned my certification late one evening after a meal of Chinese takeout. By that time, September first approached at a break-neck pace.

Ideally, my arrival in Blacktail Creek would be Saturday, the last day of August, so I could scope out the area before second impressions were required. In order to meet that deadline, I used two days of my PTO for a trip to a store for sportsmen and a camper rental company. I reserved my camper weeks ago, but Friday afternoon my scheduled pickup time would arrive. Today's goal: acquire gear.

Standing in front of a building with a log cabin façade beside a strip mall, I breathe in confidence. My sleek, matte black Tesla looks out of place surrounded by Ford and GMC trucks, and I haven't seen a single man in a suit walk past. However, camo cargo shorts appear in excess. With an online checklist in hand and an overwhelmingly large budget, I find myself standing at the center of the store, staring into the eyes of a stuffed bear.

How did my life come to this?

Stuffed animals are displayed in what equates to the adult version of a diorama. Plastic plant-life, and rocks that *might* be real act as the background for dead, taxidermized beasts. Similarly, fish decorate the crown molding, and amongst it all lies so much merchandise. Fishing poles spear the air, rising above the racks of camouflage. A wall of guns stretches toward the back. Wood signs designate areas I've never even heard of, and I realize my education in outdoor sports lacked some major points. Suddenly, the list in my hand seems insufficient.

"Can I help you, sir?" My eyes flick down to a man with a green vest stretched over his beer belly. He's a foot shorter than me, even in his utilitarian boots, and he wears a hat with the American flag sewn into the side. His name shines up from the badge on the brim of his hat. His name is Hank. Because, of course, it is.

"Uh, yeah. I need hunting stuff." God, I sound like an idiot. "A gun, some gear for camping, maybe. I'll be out for the season."

"The whole season, huh? Lucky guy like you must make a fortune. This way."

He leads me through the store, ignoring the designated paths of travel to zigzag through the surrounding racks.

"You got the proper clothes?" he asks, looking at my bespoke suit with disdain. "Can't wear that in the woods."

The list I printed had 'clothing' as a single item. I guess I assumed jeans and tennis shoes would be sufficient, but glancing around the store and the men inside it had me second-guessing myself. All the instructors in my videos wore head-to-toe camo with pops of neon orange. I owned shirts in brighter reds and shades of salmon, but never neon orange. From the panic on my face, my helpful associate began sifting through a collection of pants and shirts. According to Hank, my wardrobe needed an upgrade.

I provided my sizes; he provided a stack of camo goods that could last me a month.

"Where are you hunting at?" He asks, picking his way through the racks some more. Pinching the black radio at his shoulder, he says, "Can someone meet me in guns with a cart? With a customer."

"Blacktail Creek," I offer. More insufficient information, I learn.

"Oh, up around the crick? I hear that's some good hunting. Zone 73 or 73A?"

An associate meets us with a cart the color of his vest, and the mountain of clothes collapses in the basket as he continues our indirect path to the gun counter. The boy who dropped it off gives me a tight smile before disappearing from our vicinity. "You know your zone?"

"I'm not sure. I'm meeting some other hunters."

"Might need a muzzleloader then. We'll get you set up real good, don't worry."

The longer my time here stretched on, the more worried I became. In over my head comforted me most of the time because I learned best through baptism by fire. When I first started at the firm, my trainer and I were pinned against one another for the position. As a result, he never taught me a thing.

It was my own failures and lessons that got me to partner, and I expected hunting to be the same. Now, my heart pounded with panic over the mere shopping experience. The mountain still awaited conquering.

As we finally reached the gun counter, I'd come to the decision that Hank was knowledgeable enough. In the shopping, I'd defer to his expertise.

"Make sure I have everything I need. I'm trusting your judgment," I explain.

He grins, semi-crooked teeth on display. "We've got you covered, guy." Slapping his hand on the glass counter, the man behind the gun counter joins us. "This is my buddy, Bill."

Because, of course, it is.

"What can I do you for?" Bill asks, and my eyes dip to Hank's.

"He's going to need a muzzleloader and probably a normal long-range," Turning to me, he asks, "You want a handgun in case of bears?"

My eyes widen. In all my research, I hadn't considered bears. Hunting them had been out of the question, so their danger became a blip on the radar until now.

"Isn't there a better alternative to deter bears?"

"There's plenty of bear safety. We can get you the bear spray, the bear bells if you want 'em, and a scent-free lock box for your food. You tent camping, or you got a camper?"

"I rented a camper."

"Safer than a tent, but a bear can still tear it to shreds. Definitely gonna want that locking box."

Bill's bushy brows pinch low, but he shrugs when I look to him for confirmation. "I don't hunt. Only know guns because of Afghanistan."

I take a deep breath. "Thank you for your service."

Another awkward shrug. "So, we doing the handgun or no, son?"

"No handgun. We'll go with the sprays and bells and boxes." The overhead lights cause an ache in my head, and I try not to think about how cooked I truly am. In over my head was telling my partner that I could handle this account. We were well past that now.

"You know what you like to shoot?"

Finally, a question I could answer.

Over the past weeks, I'd learned that I liked the .243 Winchester and any version of a .270. While the sniper portion of the course had been enjoyable, I enrolled for the hunting weapons and those were my preference. Both Bill and Hank appeared surprised by my knowledge and choice, but I left the gun counter feeling like I'd earned some respect.

On and on the minutes ticked, more and more things got added to the cart. A locking Yeti cooler, a foldable micro-cot and sleeping mat in case I got stuck on the mountain overnight. Emergency gear, a hunting blind, tree stands, bugles and calls, dry bags, a hiking pack, and so much more. The list seemed never-ending and by the time I left, I was three-thousand dollars poorer and a gold member of the club.

Hank helped me to my car personally and loaded my bags like Jenga pieces. If he was surprised by the Tesla, he didn't show it. Instead, he held out his hand and shook mine.

"Pleasure doing business with you. Can't wait to see what you kill."

I smile and nod, but both feel tense, ungenuine. We shake hands, and I can't help but wonder if I was 'one of those' clients for him.

Rows of white, silver, and black trailers of all sizes emblazoned with yellow smiley faces greet me as I drive into Happy Campers rental lot. Above me, the sun is shining, and a brand new pair of Ray-Bans sit on the bridge of my nose. The polarized lenses were the only thing I bought yesterday that I didn't need any help to pick out.

Circular yellow signs denote 'Pickup Parking' in front of a large double-wide trailer with the door propped open. Climbing from my car, I make my way inside.

As I repacked my goods last night, recycling all its packaging, the excitement started to settle in. With all my gear packed, I scoured the internet for the best camp foods and subsequently learned about walking tacos and Dutch oven meals. My purchase of groceries was enough to feed an army and included the best treats to roast over a campfire. I hoped s'mores would be the breakthrough I needed for Jack Collister's tough exterior.

As the kind of man who liked to tackle things head-on, learn new skills, and prove my grit, this hunting opportunity turned into an exciting new frontier.

Inside the double-wide, business cubicles were full of friendly faces. A centered coffee table sat covered in camping magazines, and a man in

Birkenstocks moseyed over to me. A couple of ladies toward the back were having an animated conversation, smiles on their faces as they stood beside the water cooler. The laid-back energy of this place existed in direct opposition to my firm.

"How can I help you, man?"

"I made a reservation for a trailer online. Should be ready for pickup under Carter."

"The Happy Hauler, right?"

"That's the one."

"Great. Gina, over there, will help you with the paperwork," He explains, pointing to a brunette with curly hair, "Can I get your truck keys and get you all hooked up?"

"Excuse me? My truck keys?"

"Yeah, you know. To haul the Happy Hauler."

The man's smile didn't fold, even as I glared down at him with distaste. Did I look like the kind of guy who owned a pickup truck? Thinking back to my reservation, I try to imagine where it said anything about needing my own. In the pictures, every trailer was hooked up to a shiny black Dodge Ram.

"You mean it doesn't come with a truck?"

His brows pinch, but his smile doesn't dim. "No, sir. The trailer rentals are separate from trucks."

"Can you get me a truck?"

"Normally, yes, but unfortunately, our trucks are all rented out for the weekend. Can I schedule a truck for you on Monday?

Monday was the second of September, and I had no way of contacting my client to let him know of any changes in the plan. Last we spoke, I would meet him at the Moonshine Cafe in Blacktail Creek at noon on the first. I couldn't wait until Monday and ruin the relationship right out the gate. If I knew where my final destination was, none of this would matter, but as of now, I needed that truck.

"Is there any way you can get me a truck?"

"Is there a friend you can call? If not, Gina can call the local Uhaul, see if they have something fit to tow that kind of weight."

Unless my best friend was secretly a NASCAR-loving tailgater, I couldn't think of a single person in my life with a pickup truck. I'd never needed one when I could have anything delivered to my door at the touch of a finger. With the newest development, my excitement waned.

"The Uhaul will work. Will they deliver it here?"

"I'm sure there's some extra charge. Will that be—"

"That's fine. Get it here and get me hooked up."

The welcome wagon waves Gina over and explains the situation. She smiles. "All good, sugar. Easy misunderstanding. Let's go over the paperwork now, shall we?"

By the end of an hour, I have the keys to a green and orange pickup and a 'happy' hauler.

CHAPTER TWO

HUNTER

"You want the night crawlers, Joe. I'm telling you," I explain for the fifteenth time, but my regulars like to test me. I've managed to pry the can of hot-pink power bait out of his hands, but he's still reaching for it. "Bullheads like the live bait."

Though one might not be able to tell from the interaction, Joe is my favorite regular. Retired from the military, he moved out to Blacktail Creek and spent his days hunting, fishing, and shooting at beer cans in his backyard. Sunday nights, I make roast, and he comes over to eat it. We're close like that.

"You're pretty bullheaded, aren't ya? And you seem to like the night crawlers," He grumbles. It's nearly closing time, and he's spent an hour here arguing with me about this, so I would say he might be right about my stubborn streak.

Shoving the foam cup of worms into his knobby old hand, I set the power bait back on the shelf with finality. My eyes roll in their sockets at his drama, and he smiles. Power bait is fine if you're teaching your kid to fish for the first time or you want stocked trout, but an experienced angler like Joe needed to buy the night crawlers and stop whining about it.

"Fine, but if I ain't catch nothin', I'm blamin' you."

"Anything else I can find you, *sir*?" It's a taunt, and he knows it.

"Don't call me sir. I work for a living."

Joe hasn't worked since '84, but I don't say a thing about it. Clapping a hand on my back, he starts turning us toward the counter when the chimes on the door ring. Joe clocks him first, letting out a low whistle. As my eyes drag from the polished wingtip boots to the well-coiffed hair, I hear him whisper, "He ain't from 'round here, is he?"

The man looks straight at the two of us. My blond braid is slung over my shoulder, hanging free since I'm curled down for Joe to throw his arm over me. My Hunter's Hardware apron doesn't look as pretty as it did when I bought it, and nametags weren't a foregone conclusion around here. Most of us subscribed to the idea that a name was something you earned. I couldn't be givin' it away willy-nilly.

"I'm looking for Hunter." Unfortunately, this man already had it.

"That's me," I smile, stepping out from Joe's embrace. I nod to the counter to tell him I'll meet him over there. He's not in a rush and probably wants to know what Moneybags wants.

"You're Hunter? The one who can sell me the proper licensure?" His eyes skim over my very female body, and he raises a questioning eyebrow.

This was a usual occurrence. No one ever believed me when I told them I was Hunter. Probably because I was a doe-eyed, blonde-haired bombshell of a woman just like my mama. I didn't need makeup to look pretty (not that I had anything against it), and I had what my cousin Carly called 'leggy legs.' The blessings never quit coming until they learned my name was Hunter. If it would make 'em feel any better, I'd tell them about my sister Archer and our oldest brother Fischer. However, that never worked before, so I went with the proven strategy.

"Oh, you're right. One sec," I grumble. I hated hobby hunters. Flipping my hat backward and pulling the toy mustache from my pocket, I stuck it to my upper lip. "Better?"

My own eyes trail over him, and I try to act like he's not a particularly impressive specimen. This man was cut from the Devil. A head taller than me and clearly in good standing with his celebrity trainer. Even his glare was hot as hell. I wouldn't mind those green eyes on me if they weren't attached to such an entitled piece of work.

"Sure. Can you help me with a hunting license or what?"

It was at this point that Joe left a twenty on my counter for his bait and Cow Tales and disappeared out the front door. My nod acknowledged his two-finger salute. Then I turned all my energy back to Jerkoff McGee. Sauntering past him with a certain swag only a non-man with a massive ego could possess, I escorted him to the counter where we could get his license sorted out.

"You ever hunted before?" I ask, pulling up the portal.

"This is my first time."

"New hunter," I smile, whispering under my breath, "makes sense."

His lips pinch together, and he glances out the window to our left. My eyes stray to what he's looking at, thinking maybe he's checking on a dog hanging its head out his window, but no. There's no cute hound puppy ready to learn to track bears. Instead, a Uhaul rental truck is hooked up to a fifth wheel with a neon-yellow smiley face on the side. He clicked the button on his key once to confirm for himself that the ugly set of advertisements he drove was locked. Like watching a train wreck, exercised effort drags my eyes back to the screen.

"Just a hunting license or a combination?"

His blank look confirms that he's not a fisher, but he responds with, "Combination."

"Great, and one year or three?"

The anxious tap of his fingers against the counter has accelerated, and I try to remain professional as he takes his sweet time dissecting my question like a complicated math problem. That stone jaw ticks. He's clearly the kind of guy who only makes calculated moves. The stick must be so far up his rear that he can't bend without breaking.

"Why would anyone want to do this three years in a row?" He asks with exasperation in his voice. "One is fine."

It's not personal. He's a city boy, through and through. I'm a country girl by blood. He doesn't know what's good for him. He'll be back to his normal comforts in no time, or he'll learn.

"Now, what about permits? You need any of those?"

"I don't know. Do you need a permit to shoot a deer?"

"Depends on the weapon. Depends on the deer," I shrug, waiting for him to answer my question.

"Listen, I'm only here doing this because my client doesn't trust a man who has never killed his own dinner. I know I need a license and a tag for the animal I kill. Can't you make the decisions? Give me what I need?"

"What do you plan to kill your dinner with?" I ask.

"I have a .243 Winchester and a 50 caliber muzzleloader."

I add the proper permits, skimming through the list to ensure he won't need anything else. I'm a bit confused about why he's telling me about guns during archery season, so I give him the opportunity to correct me.

"Do you need an archery tag?"

"No, I think a gun is good enough."

"Are you sur—"

"Positive. Please get me the proper tags."

A couple of side-by-sides swing into the parking lot, and I watch the Collister Crew disperse. They like to play their music loud, but they're respectful of the road laws, and they turn it down when they pull in. I've got a freezer of bagged ice outside, and the littlest Collister picks up two bags while Jack and his brother, Wyatt, slip into the store. Lane is there, too. His new girl sat beside him, but he didn't get out of his UTV. Instead, he hands a new girl in the back a wad of cash with his instructions. They descend on my shop like a group of hyenas.

Hunter's Hardware wasn't like the mercantile a little further down the way. I didn't carry any grocery-style foods, only a single row of chips and candies at the front counter and a cooler of single-serve soda and beer. Outside, you could buy ice or air, but it would cost you. Otherwise, the place was filled with anything you might need to hunt, fish, or fix a camper trailer. Like whatever box store Proper License Boy bought his hiking pants from, but on a much smaller and more niche scale. My shop had saved many a person's day in its time.

"Are you hunting anything special?" I ask, after putting the diphead down for general deer and elk.

"*Deer,*" He enunciates as if I'm slow.

Since he's a dunce, I add a couple of extra specialty deer tags so that his bases are covered and finish up in the portal. "ID."

He hands me his license, and I enter the information, ignoring his rich boy name. Nash? Seriously.

"That will be $356 even."

He doesn't even blink at the number, and that's enough to tell me I want this guy gone. His paperwork prints, and I fold it into an orange plastic case before sliding it across the table. His tapping fingers snatch it as he turns toward the door.

"Have a good day!" I say in my sweetest voice while I wiggle my fingers in his direction. He stalks away, exiting without another word. Luckily, none of The Collisters seemed to notice our disappointing exchange and my smile was genuine by the time Jack sidles up to the counter.

He's not a year-round regular like Joe, but Jack and I have learned about one another over the years. His family comes to Blacktail Creek often during the summer, and I don't see him leave until the bulk of hunting season is over. Since they've been coming here for years, we know one another pretty well. He's even offered to show me his hunting spot—a pretty big deal for hunters everywhere.

Today, he grabbed some extra tips for his bow and a cold Diet Coke for his wife. I ring those items up before little Colter pops his head in to shout about the two bags of ice, and then Wyatt adds a handful of snacks to the counter beside his bottle of scent blocker.

"You huntin' this year?" Wyatt asks as I add his goods to the tab.

They all pay together because Jack has Warren Buffet type money, and his brothers work directly for him. Lane does, too, but the new girl in the cut-off shorts refuses to let Jack pay, laying down Lane's cash for the bag of sour candy and tall boys in her hand.

"I might try for an elk. The freezer's looking a little thin," I say as I make change for her. It tended to get a little thin when picky old men like Joe wanted elk steaks every Sunday. If I could get him to eat the deer, it wouldn't be so lean, but I can only trick him about half the time.

"Well, you're always welcome at base camp," Jack adds.

"You know that I live here, right? That I probably have my own spots that are just as good as yours?"

Both men put their hands up like I've got a gun trained on them.

"Someone offend your sensibilities today, Hunter?" Jack asks.

"Yeah, you know we don't just invite you up because you're pretty, right?" Wyatt jokes, pointing at his lip. I ignore the heat in my cheeks as I slip the mustache off and into my pocket.

"That's clear enough," the new girl agrees, pointing at the mounted 5x5 rack on the back wall. She tosses long, blonde hair like my own over her shoulder, and I decide I like her.

"Sorry. Joe decided to razz me a little too hard this morning, I guess."

I'm not sure what causes me to lie, but as I peek out the window at Nash from Denver, pity seeps into my bones. Leaving the counter behind, I walk out the door with The Collisters as they assure me I'm still welcome, even when I'm feeling a bit feisty.

Little Colter sprints towards my knees, wrapping his arms around my waist tight before begging, "Can Hunter please come up to camp this season? Please, pops?"

Wyatt smiles, swinging the boy into his arms and detaching him from my legs. "Hunter will join us if she wants to. Ain't that right, Hunter?"

"I'm thinking about it, Colt."

His excitement bubbles over, and he screams with joy so loud I almost don't hear Jack over it. While I was busy smiling at a little kid, wondering when it would be my turn, Big Money walked over to greet Jack with an outstretched hand.

"He's early," Lane says.

"This your ugly rig?" Jack asks like he knows the condescending Hollywood-Chris-wannabe.

Now, if I were a better person, I'd mind my business, head inside, and close up shop. Instead of pretending to enjoy the late afternoon sun and secretly eavesdropping, I might head off to join Joe at the river and listen to him complain about my choice of bait. Rather than listening in as Jack and Nash talked about what they would hunt, I would sit at home and think about adopting a dog. Yet, this was a small town, and drama didn't surface often.

As I listen in, keeping my head tilted toward the sun and a hand on the door handle, I learn that these two know each other and Jack is the client Mr. Cash-Dollars wants to impress. I huff a quiet laugh when I realize he's going to be really impressive hunting during archery season without an archery tag.

Turning away, I hear the moment that Jack enlightens Nash about his situation.

"Got your archery tag? Ready to go?"

"Is it not gun season?"

"Not for another thirty days, my guy," Wyatt says. His tone is forever playful.

Those fancy leather booties come screeching across the gravel, but I move quicker. Into the door, the lock is already engaged. I'm sliding down the blinds when he shouts, "Wait! Hunter, please? I need an archery permit!"

I show him the face of my watch through the window, flicking off the lights with my free hand. "We closed two minutes ago. You'll have to come back another day."

"Seriously? It's a piece of paper. Print it. I have cash."

"No-can-do, Bones." I flip the sign so my door says closed and hear The Collisters laughing. He grunts with irritation and kicks the gravel beside the front door. I ignore his theatrics as I finish closing up. Slipping out the back door, I ignore the prick of his eyes on me as I walk around the front to my dirt bike.

The Collisters have already fled, though I'm sure they would be back soon. After inviting such a precious guest, I'm sure they wouldn't leave him here all night.

"Do you know what you're costing me right now?" He shouts, but I ignore him as I stomp my kick starter to drown out his whining. "I'm already thousands of dollars into this hole. I told you what I needed, and you—"

My bike roars to life, and relief floods my system.

"Listen," I snap over the rumble of my bike. "Earlier, you were paying me to listen to your plight. I'm off the clock now, Bones. So unless you're pulling out Benjamins, I'm done for the day."

I never actually gave him the opportunity to pay me for my time. Instead, I rev my bike, turn onto the street, and drive away from the worst day I've had since my parents moved to Arizona.

CHAPTER THREE

NASH

Blacktail Creek could burn for all I cared. Not only did Hank fail to mention the necessary license, but I was already halfway to this god-forsaken place when the podcast mentioned it. Nearly twenty miles later, the same podcast died out entirely as I lost service completely. Miraculous didn't even begin to explain the peeling billboard that read, "Hunting License and Tags—see Hunter."

Since I'd passed the mercantile first, I stopped in to ask after said Hunter, but the lady wouldn't tell me a thing unless I bought something. So, with one of those personal fans you can fill with water in hand, she explained that Hunter could be found further down the road at Hunter's Hardware. She said it like I was thick at first, but one glance at my shirt and she tacked on a kind, "Bless your heart."

The actual shop, more like a well-kept shack, exceeded my expectations when I walked in. Neat rows of hunting, camping, and fishing gear boosted my spirits. I knew I was in the right place. Then, I had to go and offend Hunter, *the girl*. The gorgeous girl with blue eyes the color of a summer sky. She looked ridiculous when she flipped her hat and stuck a fake mustache on her upper lip, but she handled business like a professional. Until she didn't.

Now, stranded in the parking lot of her little shack, with another poor impression made on my client, I didn't know what to do. Wait her out, maybe? My eyes strayed to my trailer. After driving so long, exhaustion wore me down. The mere concept of backing that thing onto the road to search for an overnight campsite on a weekend made the decision for me.

If she didn't want to help me, I'd wait until she did.

A pounding on my trailer door woke me from my slumber. Disoriented from sleep, I fell out of my bed. The wildest dream about a blonde-haired witch still sang through my mind as I stumbled past the bathroom and to the door. Another *pound, pound, pound* slammed on the rickety door, and I struggled to unlock it with my eyes half-shut.

From the trailer's tilt the door swung open quick, and my visitor hopped out of the way. Outdoor light streamed into the dim interior of the trailer, and the sight of pine trees reminded me where I was.

Squinting down at my visitor, I grumble, "Can I help you?"

"She ain't coming in today, and you ain't supposed to park here overnight."

"Who?" I ask, my mind still spinning. The queen bed was comfortable enough, but it was not a therapeutic, spine-supportive masterpiece like my bed at home.

"Hunter. She won't be here today, so you ought to scoot."

He points off into the woods, past a rickety, old 'For Sale' sign made out of a pallet. As I take in the man's appearance, his words process in my groggy mind. "You mean Hunter won't come in at all?"

A number of things confounded me about that. I hadn't taken a Sunday off since I started at my firm, so to hear this backwoods girl could, inspired a level of jealousy I hated to admit. The other piece that didn't click was how this random man knew where she would be. Why did he know her schedule so intimately? The gray hair seemed a bit on the old side for him to be her father.

"It's Sunday." He replies like that's a reasonable answer. Was I in some bible-banging town where Sunday remained a holy day?

"And?"

"And on Sunday, she goes fishing."

"Right," *of course she does.*

"So, you gonna move that ugly truck or what?"

I lean against the doorway and give it a thought. I doubted this old man's words about parking here, but getting a ticket from a forest ranger wouldn't be a good look, either. A plan sticks in my mind.

"You look like you need some coffee. Why don't you come in and we chat about it?

"I ain't comin' in there unless you got pants on, son."

A glance down my body, and I realize I'm dressed in nothing but a white tee and boxers. Turning away from the door, I leave it open.

"Easily remedied," I call out, hustling to my room at the head of the trailer. The whole thing rocks with our steps as I get dressed for the day, and the local guy finds his way inside.

"How long was you huntin' for?"

"The season," I call back. The assumption that hunting season was like basketball or football season left me with the hope that I could win an early game and dip when I was finished. However, my boss was

34

prepared to have me off-grid for a few months. I didn't like being away from the office for long, but I would prove myself come hell or high water.

"But what season? Archery? Or are you staying when guns open up?"

When I make my way back down the steps, my visitor is sat at the breakfast nook, which is still tucked in tight to the kitchen. The man at Happy Campers taught me how to use all the buttons, and when he toured the camper with all the pull-outs set up, it was spacious. Since I kept everything pulled in and slept in it as is last night, my guest looked a little crammed.

"You know, I didn't get your name," I tell him, dumping some extra grounds into the machine. The man looked like the type who liked his coffee strong, maybe with a cigarette on the side.

"Yeah. That's cause you didn't earn it."

"Well, how about an exchange then?" With the coffee pot set and the scent of black drip filling the enclosed space, I turn to face my guest and lean against the counter. "I'm Nash Carter. You are?"

"Joe."

"Short for Joseph?"

"No."

We sit in awkward silence for a minute; the only sounds are the dull chirps of birds outside and the *tink, tink, tink* of the coffee dripping against the glass carafe. While I'm waiting him out, playing a corporate power move I'd perfected, he's quietly staring me down like he can uncover all my secrets from a look. His eyes narrow slightly, and I crack first.

"Where's Hunter?"

Joe laughs. The booming sound jolts his body and shakes the trailer. The coffee sloshes gently. I fold my arms over my chest. In the past, my partners have said that I'm impossible to ignore when my arms are crossed. The interns whisper about my 'Intimidation Mode.' Unfortunately, Joe's hard exterior isn't for show.

"Now, why would I tell you that, City Boy?"

His nickname for me chafes because I gave him my name. He could have called me Nash or Mr. Carter even, but he chose to point out the one thing that set me apart from him and Hunter alike. And the way he said it felt derogatory like he was calling me the scum of the earth and not just 'City Boy.'

Pouring the coffee, I pull creamer from the cooler full of ice and offer it wordlessly. A shake of his head has me turning for the sugar, but he declines that, too, taking the mug as it is. Meanwhile, I add a splash of the creamer and a cube of sugar without issue. He already thinks I'm soft, so there's no reason to change now.

"I need a permit, and she should have given it to me yesterday."

"Well, you ain't gonna see her today. She's out at her fishing hole."

"And where is that?"

"That girl feeds me steak and potatoes every Sunday evening while you showed up outta nowhere with something to prove buzzin' around you like flies. Why on God's green earth would I tell you where she's at?"

"I can think of a hundred reasons why," I say, pulling the hundred-dollar bill from my wallet and laying it beside the sink. Joe's brows furrow, and he scoffs.

"Your money ain't good here, boy." In the next breath, he gulps down the rest of his scalding coffee and stands from the table. "You'll do good to remember that girl you're underminin'; she runs this town."

He walks toward the door, and I'm torn between groveling for information and letting him leave.

Hunter will come back to the shop eventually, but if it wasn't today, I wouldn't be ready when Mr. Collister came back for me. Irritation spikes through me as I hustle toward the old man.

"What'll it take for you to tell me where the fishing hole is?"

I never should have trusted his crooked smile.

CHAPTER FOUR

HUNTER

Crisp dew clung to long stalks of grass beside the trail as I carried my fishing gear down to the stream. The scent of fresh sap and moss hewed to the damp air, overriding the old garlicky bait smell adhered to my tackle box. On the bank of the river, I unfold my bifold chair and hang my legs over the rock edge. Laying my pole on the ground, I pop open my tackle box and peruse the many flies and baits. On the creek, I liked two small weights about six inches above my hook and worms for bait.

Casting my line into the water, I listened to the sounds of nature surrounding me. Early morning light illuminated the sky, but the sun hadn't peeked over the mountain ridge yet. Soon enough, I'd have the best view in Blacktail as the sun streamed through the trees like strands of golden webbing.

My fishing hole was public knowledge, but only those of a very specific community knew exactly where it was. The Over-65 crew within Blacktail and I knew of its existence, but only I could get down close enough to the water for it to be any good. As the youngest resident of Blacktail Creek, that didn't leave many people who didn't know where I spent my Sunday mornings. Those same locals protected my tradition from visitors who may want to bang down my shop door.

Pinching my pole between my knees, I dug into the paper bag tucked inside my tackle box. Once a month, a chilled food truck came through, and I bought microwaveable breakfast sandwiches with ooey-gooey, melty American cheese and a package of sticky buns the truck driver's wife makes.

One bite into the egg, sausage, and cheese and a hum of approval worked its way out of me. Nothing topped a quiet Sunday morning with a warm breakfast sandwich. The salty, savory flavors blended on my tongue as I watched the water's edge.

I loved watching the water churn around rocks, adding a hazy white color to the otherwise clear water. About fifteen feet upstream, dozens of stones stuck out of the surface, letting the flow cut around them before evening out where I fished. Even though the water looked calm and clear here, it was deceptively deep. My line sunk into the water and seemed to disappear. The only hint of its existence was the soft tension of the current.

Housing my sandwich, I brush the crumbs on my jeans before drawing my line in and recasting. I understood the anglers with the patience of an immortal god, but it couldn't be me. I liked to throw my line wide, pause and reel, pause and reel. The activity kept my mind blank better than the sound of the water or the scents of morning air. Plus, it caught me my first fish, and action became a tradition.

As I reel the line in a few inches, I feel a bite. Snapping on the line, I start to reel it in. My mind jumps to the idea of a large trout based on how it tugs. My pole curves into the likeness of a C, and I release a bit of the tension on my line. That seems to do the trick as I finish reeling the beast in, dragging it straight onto the rocky shore.

My pole falls to the side as I drag the fish up by the line and smile. About eleven inches in length, it's barely in the edible size range, but the bright colors of its scales tell me it's healthy. Pulling it off the hook with a practiced hand, I toss it in a cooler full of ice to keep it fresh. If I can catch another around the same size, I might be able to convince Joe that fish sounds better than red meat.

I'm baiting my hook when I hear the snap of a branch behind me. Swinging around to face the trail, I peer up the steep incline. It's possible that Joe felt lonely and wanted to sit in broody silence while I fished, but no one emerged from the shadowed trail. Turning back to my hook, I held the wriggly worm steady as I stabbed the hook through. This time, another crashing sound is accompanied by a hushed curse, and I turn toward the sound.

Tumbling through the underbrush fifteen feet to the north of the trail is the last person I expected to see. I cast my line into the river, ignoring him.

"You better not be here."

"I need that damn permit."

"Sucks for you, Bones."

Hyperawareness of his approaching steps creates tension in my shoulders; I try to focus on the soft pull on my line from the water. He stops a step behind me, panting like he hiked a steep incline rather than half-stumbling downhill.

"Hunter, please? If you get me the permit, I'll be out of your hair."

I ignore him, dropping back into my chair and slowly reeling my line in. My peace fled the moment he arrived, but I tried to draw it back in like the fish. Slow and steady, I keep my eyes focused on the water, my ears tuned to the sounds of the forest coming to life.

"Wow," He whispers, making my own goals impossible.

My eyes stray from the water to his face, and the golden sheen of the sun bathes his muscular figure. He's not looking at me, nor the river, but the sky. The streams of gilded light skim the treetops, carving a path through them and glinting off the river's surface. Suddenly, my chest cracked open, and vulnerability seeped out. Turns out he's capable of slow appreciation. His lips parted at the view as a hawk called from above, diving through the beams of light. He wasn't looking at me, but I knew he saw me for the first time in that moment. He knew me inside and out now, but he didn't even know it.

Forcing my eyes back to the water, I reel my line in slightly. My heartbeat bumps and stutters, but I ignore it. I'm here to fish. It's a normal Sunday. I didn't see Bones as attractive. He didn't see my sacred space in all its glory. Everything was fine.

I absolutely don't hear him shuffle forward to the edge or feel his arm brush mine as he takes a seat beside me. Pulling my line from the water, I recast, watching the wriggly end of my hook plop back into the water.

"I'm sorry about yesterday," He says. His voice is soft, but my unwillingness to hear him overrides his words.

"Be quiet. You'll scare the fish."

Am I over-correcting for the moment of weakness? Yes. Do I care? No.

The man breaks the silence maybe forty seconds later, "I didn't mean to offend you. You weren't what I expected."

I hush him, ignoring his sigh. He stays beside me quietly. I reel and recast twice before he speaks again.

"I'm not usually the kind of guy who underestimates women. I promise."

"Didn't think you were." It's a lie. I absolutely think he is. Otherwise, why assume a girl couldn't be named Hunter or that she wasn't fit to sell you a hunting license? Why look at her life's work with absolute disdain? He was a guy's guy, and those were the worst kind.

"You know I can tell you're lying, right?"

I bristle. About to turn and give him a what for, I feel a bite. Snapping back to my reel, I set the hook. This fish is bigger than the first; I can feel it. The pole starts to curve, and City Boy smiles.

"Did you catch a fish?"

I ignore him, focusing on bringing the thing in. It fights, and I give it a bit of line before reeling it in further. It tugs, I yank. Nash chatters at me with excitement, watching me like I'm the New York Stock Exchange or whatever finance bros like him find interesting. He's quietly cheering for me like I'm a sports match.

"You got this. You can reel it in. Jeez, that's massive."

The fish pops from the water, and I toss my pole into his lap, pulling the line up from the water's edge to see the trout. Same healthy color as his friend; this guy is well over a foot. He fights and dangles on the line as I try to get my hand around him gently.

"That's insane," Bones whispers, watching carefully as I pull the hook from the fish's mouth. Popping open the cooler, I drop him beside his friend, and the sense of achievement curls over me.

With two fish down, I didn't need to catch anymore, but the morning remained cool. The last few Sundays, I didn't get a single bite, but I didn't mind. For me, fishing wasn't about the catch; it was about the peace. I liked the moment when the sun started to warm the Earth, and the scent of the river washed over me in the same cadence as the surrounding sounds. It was like church for Miss Mabel from the mercantile but without the walls and uncomfortable wooden pews.

"You're incredible," my visitor whispers and that peace shatters.

Gathering up my gear, I ignore his sudden appreciation of me and chalk it up to what it truly is: kiss-assery. He wants me to open up shop and print him his proper ticket. He probably expects me to sell him a bow, too. Poor guy doesn't seem to understand, I won't do it.

He offers to carry my pole for me, but I don't let him. Nothing he says or does will make me change my mind about working today. I take Sundays off. Mornings fishing, afternoons catching up on reality TV, and evenings with Joe. A method to my madness.

At the top of the hill, my pickup sits beside the road. Cherry-red paint has grown dull with age, but she's still in great shape. I drop the tailgate, tossing in my pole, cooler, and tackle box. The foldable chair comes off my shoulder and slides in behind them.

"So, I'll meet you at the shop then?"

He's still here? The too-loud slam of the tailgate makes him jump, and I scoff. Going around the side of the truck, I ignore the small-town hospitality urging me to help the guy out. He's right there, opening up my door like some kind of post-war house husband.

"Please?" He begs.

Why was I so soft-hearted?

"Fine." I huff. "But only so you'll stop derailing my day. Get in so we can get this over with."

"Thank you."

"Don't thank me yet."

He hustles around the truck as I spin the handle to roll down the window. The truck's air conditioner stopped working last summer, and Donny gave up on fixing it. When he was a little younger, he'd go into town for the parts he needed, but now everything was online, and no one delivered here. So, the cross breeze was the best I could get. Moneybags seems confused by the wheel-crank for the window, but as I put the truck in drive, he figures it out.

Driving down the dusty path, I stop when we reach the pavement. Checking both directions, I pull out onto the road and flip the truck around in the direction of the shop. It's not a far walk from here to Hunter's Hardware. On fishing days, I always bring the rig. My house is about a mile up the road, anyway. With the windows down and an old Conway Twitty tape playing in the background, I settle into comfortable silence until a masculine clearing of a throat reminds me that I have company.

Eyes on the road, I ask, "How'd you find me anyhow?"

The only other time I'd been interrupted at my special fishing hole was when my family still lived in the area. Archer used to follow me around like younger sisters do, but I didn't mind. Ever since they left, I spent my Sunday mornings alone.

"Can't say."

"Joe, then?" There weren't many options left around here.

My dad, Hunter Sr., burned out from city life and moved us all to this tiny little town in the middle of nowhere when I was barely eighteen. He opened the store and raised me and my two siblings to adulthood. Then, my mom got sick. The drives to the hospital became more frequent. Then, she needed specialists for her particular brand of autoimmune disease. So, they moved to Arizona, where they could get the care they needed, and my two siblings went with them.

Dad offered to help me move, too, but I'd already fallen in love with Blacktail Creek. Learned to fish and hunt. Found out I preferred the quiet life, and there was Sam. Kind of thought he'd be my forever, but turns out cowboys don't know how to settle down.

"Now that you ask, I'm not sure I even got their name. Only a tip about a cherry-red truck. And a trail that's impossible to find."

Definitely Joe. But I'll deal with him later.

"And you believed them?"

"Everyone around here seems so trustworthy." He smirks, and his eyes feel like laser beams warming the side of my face. It feels like he's teasing me for swindling him out of his archery permit yesterday, but that can't be right because I double-checked with him.

"I bet you trust whatever hoity-toity, suit-monkey boss you got, too. He says you're a team, and you believe it even though you're the one stranded on this mountain, thousands of dollars in a hole, without a clue about what you're doing."

"I have a clue," He argues.

"Just need to get ten more."

"Probably eleven."

Before I can respond, Hunter's Hardware appears around the corner. Pulling into the gravel parking, I leave the truck in its usual spot. I don't wait for him to hop out or get my door. I don't say a thing. Instead, I take my keys and unlock the front door, flipping one of two lights as we walk in.

The big bar lights flicker on, warming up slowly and bathing the room in dim, fluorescent light. The shop remains how I left it, down to the twist in my apron by the back door. While I boot up the computer, Nash catches up. As he walks through the shop door, I tell him to lock the door and he fumbles with the finicky lock and jumps at the loud *click*.

"Don't want anyone getting any ideas," I say by way of explanation. Despite what Prince Deep-Pockets thinks, I keep my shop closed on Sundays. Everyone needs a break sometimes, even those who love what they do.

The permit is simple work. We pull up his information with his ID, add the permit, he pays, and he's good to go. Afterward, the situation becomes complicated.

He's got a hand on the door handle when he turns back to me. His teeth clench in his grimace as he pleads, "You don't happen to have a bow, do you?"

CHAPTER FIVE

NASH

Despite the months of education, I'm lost. Hunting is completely out of my wheelhouse. A fact that's exacerbated by nearly walking out of Hunter's shop without a bow. I try to make my grimace a grin, but she knows better.

"You're hopeless," She mutters, stomping out from her spot behind the counter. Her hand fists in my shirt, knuckles scraping across my chest through the fabric, and she drags me to the back of the shop. There are three bows on hooks against the wall. She releases my shirt and points at all three, "Pick one."

I grab the one on the left, preparing to lift it off the wall, when she groans. I glance back at her, and she's rolling her eyes at me. I *really* like those eyes.

"What?"

"Not that one."

"Why not?"

"Do you think you can manage a seventy-pound draw? That's what? Like a third of what you weigh? Pick a different one."

I don't know what a seventy-pound draw means, but I leave the bow on the hook and look between the two other bows. Since she didn't like the first choice, I moved to the one on the right. It's smaller, must not be as difficult. She slaps my hand out of the way.

"That one's for a child."

I scoff, crossing my arms over my chest to look down at her. My 'Intimidation Mode' may not have worked on Joe, but as I glare down at my newest barrier to success, I hope for the best.

"If the center option was my only option, why did you tell me to choose?"

She shrugs, "I wanted to see if you had any chance."

"Any chance of what?"

"Actually managing to kill a deer this season." She crosses her arms over her own chest, mirroring my body language.

"How does my choice in bow have anything to do with my ability to hunt?"

"Oh, you're right," She mocks, "The weapon doesn't matter at all, nor does your ability to use it. Go ahead, pick up the first one."

"No." For some reason, her order caused me to back up a step. Somehow, she turned my own tactics against me, and I felt cornered.

"Do it. I have a target out back. Let's see you shoot it."

"No, I'll take the center one."

"Oh, c'mon. Pick the big bow. Don't be a chicken."

"I'm not being a chicken. I want something sufficient for the job."

"*Bock! Bock!*"

Her arms come to make tiny wings under her pits, and I snap. Pulling the bow from the wall, I turn her by the shoulder and push her toward the back entrance. She pulls herself away from me, shaking off my hand and leading the way with a smug smile.

Because I'm in hell, there's a hay target with a red dot at the center about thirty yards from the door. She walks to a brick lying on the ground. Practice arrows lay in a raised planter.

"This is twenty yards. It's a good practice length."

She demonstrates with ease drawing the bow with smooth concentration. The brightly tipped projectile hits the target slightly off-center. She hands me the bow with an order.

"Make the shot."

I was under no impression that my Lord of the Rings marathon-watching skills prepared me for this moment, but I knocked the arrow. There were these odd fingers like a basting brush, and it felt clumsy to shove the arrow through. I almost release it before I can line it up properly, and I bite back my embarrassment. My cheeks heat, but I managed to get it together. This bow must be nicer than the ones in movies because there's some kind of wheel and a finger hold to help. With my hands in the proper grips, I draw back the arrow. Or, at least, I try to. Just like I try emulating Hunter's smooth aim.

The heavy resistance takes focus to pull back, and I thank my trainer suddenly for the functional training he forced me into. With great effort, I get the bow prepared to shoot, directing it up from the ground and toward the target. *Carters win*, I remind myself.

My arms shake from the effort, but I smirk in Hunter's direction. She's biting back a smile, and I can't help but feel like I've won something. Hubris overtakes me, and I release the arrow without looking.

In my head, it sailed through the air, sinking into the center of the target and proving my prowess. In reality, I overextended my front arm, and the string scraped against my forearm, instantly cutting and bruising the skin as the arrow clattered to the ground a foot ahead of me. I shouted in pain, and the bow fell to the ground as I tried to inspect the burning skin.

Worse, Hunter laughed. She was as girly as they came. A lilting, musical laugh floated out of her at my pain. She wheezed slightly as she walked toward me.

"You should have seen your smug face," She giggles. "You were so sure of yourself."

Her sweet hands wrapped around my wrist, and she inspected the wounds. She squeezed a few places in my arm, and when she hit a tender spot, I hissed. Her laughter fell away at my sound of pain, and a droplet of blood from one of the minor cuts dripped to the dirt between us.

Under her breath, she whispers, "You really showed me."

She drags me away from the forgotten bow and back toward the door. In the shop, she sets me on her stool, leaving me there. Another drop of blood drips down my forearm and the wounded flesh throbs. No worse than my wounded ego, though. When she returns, she carries a little red tin labeled Coca-Cola. She opens it to reveal first-aid supplies.

"Oh, you don't have to—"

"Hush. It's my fault you're hurt."

A spritz of something in an unmarked bottle hits the open wounds, and I clench my teeth against the burn. Must have been alcohol-based.

"A warning next time," I whisper through clenched teeth.

Her eyes flash up to mine, and I realize for the first time how close we are. I'm on the stool, my legs spread wide, and she stands between them. I can see her arguing with herself. She wants to snap at me, but her focus returns to the wounds. She carefully cleans them, keeping her touch gentle but thorough. She patches up the worst of my cuts, and then her awareness of our proximity matches mine. She steps away.

"All better." Her words are barely a whisper, but they seem to echo through the quiet space. In a different world, I might admit to myself how beautiful she is, that the potential to like this girl existed within me. In this reality, I choked.

"I should probably buy the center one. If I broke the one outside, I can pay for it too."

Hunter didn't say anything. Instead, her brows knit together, and she stomped out the back door. The bow looked fine, and she hung it back on the shelf, getting me the one I needed. I wasn't sure why her silence felt so uncomfortable or why I wanted her to speak with me, tease me.

She kept quiet as she gathered up the new bow and a set of arrows. She snatched up an arm guard and some other equipment I might need and dragged it all over the counter, tallying each item as she went. I must have said her name ten times before she finally spoke.

"You know, it doesn't matter what bow you buy if you still can't hit the target."

"I'll practice. It will be fine."

She huffs, reading off my total. My card slides through her machine, and then our business concludes. But I stay, just standing there.

Can I really do this? Can I really kill my own dinner? I start to question myself as Jack's concerns, and subsequently Hunter's, catch up with me. When I had a gun on my side, I was confident. Now? Drawing that bow was harder than expected. I didn't get anywhere near the target, and I'd injured myself.

The answer comes to me in the form of an angry blonde. She moved across the room toward the door, throwing it open with a flourish and a glare. It's an obvious dismissal, but I ignore her and my bags on the counter. Instead, I say, "Hunting Guide. Be my hunting guide."

CHAPTER SIX

HUNTER

He's delusional. Like, lost his marbles, delusional. Not only had this man questioned my name, given me trouble about his license, made demands, and hunted me down to drag me into work on my day off, but now he wanted me to teach him to hunt?

The low light of the shop highlights the muscles in his arms as he leans against the counter. Nash has this capacity to look confident, like he belongs, even though nothing about him screams 'customer of Hunter's Hardware.' Even though he's making his most outrageous request yet.

"Absolutely not." Does he have any clue how much time a hunting guide spends with their trainee? The bond that comes from hunting within a party? The spiritual experience it is when you achieve your goal for the first time? He asked too much of me. No way.

"Please? I'll pay you. Three thousand, half now, half when I make the kill."

My eyes bulge. Three grand? Hunter's Hardware dealt in hundreds often but never thousands. Since my parents paid off the house before they moved, leaving it to me, my biggest personal bills didn't even pass that number.

"Three too low? I'll double it."

Now, I'm choking. Literally coughing at the prospect of six thousand dollars. Six thousand dollars in a town like this would do a lot of good. I could repave the road in front of Miss Mabel's house, put a new façade on the shop, and replace the AC in my truck. He must be high. There's no way he's just carrying around a check worth six thousand dollars.

"You're nuts," My head shakes back and forth in disbelief. The door remains open, but it's the only thing holding me up. He's crazy. It's true about the chemtrails in the cities because nothing else explains his complete lack of judgment, "I can't be your hunting guide."

He tucks his hands in his pockets, smirking at me. "You drive a hard bargain, but seventy-five hundred is the best I can do."

My mouth opens and closes like a fish. He's got me on his line, for sure. Trying to reel in my own thoughts is like fighting a cat with a low-weight line. My mind snaps.

"I can't take your money."

"Please, you will be providing me with a much-needed service. You said so yourself."

"I'm not qualified."

"You can't keep me safe and help me *bag* a deer?"

He was already learning, and it made my head spin. Who even taught him that? When did he pick up that terminology, and what else did he know since stepping foot in my town? It was clear Nash was a motivated guy. He would be a good student.

"Of course I can. But I—"

"Oh, so it's because you're scared?"

My teeth grind. He's such an ass. More likely to die on the mountain than kill anything. But he's baited me, and I'm falling for it.

Crossing my arms over my chest, I saunter in his direction with my eyes narrowed. The door slams closed with a clang. "If I do this, you don't question me about anything. I'm there to keep you safe and get you an animal. My word is law."

"You got it."

I expected more fighting about it, but his mouth is set in a perma-smile.

"And you still pay half now, half when we gain an animal for you."

"Not a problem, but one last stipulation."

I wait, saying nothing.

"No one knows about this deal."

"Do you know how close we're going to be the whole time? They're going to know."

"Not if you pretend we're dating," He murmurs, brushing a stray hair from my face. I slap his hand away.

"No. I won't *lie* to The Collisters. They're good people."

"Then don't lie. We'll tell them I pursued you; I liked your stubbornness—none of that's untrue. I convinced you to take them up on their offer to hunt with us so I could get to know you better."

"And what about the part where we go off together every morning to find an animal? The part where I'm stuck to your side like glue, even at camp, making sure you don't ruin my beautiful environment?"

He steps closer, brushing his hand down my shoulder, and I curse the prickle of awareness.

"We're dating; of course, we want to spend all our time together."

"And if I can't pretend to like you? Since you're insufferable?"

"You're doing fine right now." His voice has dropped to a whisper, and my heart flutters. The effects of him make no sense. He's annoying. I hate him. I take a big step back.

"Ten grand. If I have to pretend to like you, lie to good people, and make sure you don't die on the mountain, I better make out like a bandit." I hold out my hand.

His palm slides against mine, and that infuriating smirk materializes. "Deal."

My breath whooshes from my lungs, discomfort swamping me, weighing me down like the heat of a humid summer day. Either I just made the easiest ten grand of my life or the biggest mistake. Only time will tell.

CHAPTER SEVEN

NASH

When Hunter meets The Collisters and me a few hours later, I admit I might have made a mistake. She was radiant in her jeans and t-shirt this morning, to a degree that was unfair. Now, breathing challenged me. The head-to-toe camo? A wire-frame pack slung over her shoulder, a bow over the other? Hunter was in her element, and it made her impossible to ignore.

"You're drooling, city-slicker," Wyatt whispers with a chuckle. With a wink, he swings Hunter into a side hug, telling her how excited his son would be that she made up her mind. He offers to take her bag, and she glares. Her eyes look as sharp as the pain of my arm feels.

When they reach the group, she says, "Sorry I'm late. Had to give Joe the keys to the shop. Then we argued about his payment in Cow Tales. He wouldn't let me leave until I ordered a second box for delivery this week."

The Collisters chuckle at this, but I'm still staring like a dope.

"Want to ride with us or Nash-Money over here?" Wyatt asks her, and I can see the moment she realizes she has to come with me. Disappointment makes a flash appearance before her eyes dull with the force of her smile.

"As fun as breaking road laws with you two sounds, I think I'll take my chances with Nash."

Her eyes land on mine, and I'm sucked in. To those outside of us, it probably looks like we're having a moment, but to me, I know she's faking it. Tiny lines pinch beside her eyes, her lips are slightly thinner than when she smiles for real. I offer my arm, and her hand slips in the crook of my elbow. She lets me load her things into the back of the truck, and I open her door for her.

A glance at The Collisters shows me it's working. A sense of respect wafts from Jack. He likes that I treat women right. Wyatt's head tilts to the side as he sizes us up. Hunter winks at him with a grin, and I hustle around to my side.

We're quiet the whole drive. I didn't download any music before I left the city, and the stations are crackly at best, so the cab is quiet. Hunter's eyes are on the passing trees, enjoying the streaks of green as I keep speed with the side-by-side racing ahead. She hums when we pull onto a dirt road and slow to a crawl. The trailer bumps along behind the truck, kicking up dust. Soon enough, the tree cover thickens, and one side of the trail drops into a stream. We pull to the side at one point for a truck that's leaving, the horns of their animal peeking up from the bed of their truck. Then, we take another turn. The truck seems to work harder from the climb, and we go slow. Deep potholes litter the dirt road, throwing us around even in the cab. When we break the top of the hill, a clearing opens up.

Jack spins the UTV into the circle and points toward the open spot on the left. Three other trailers make the other sides of a semicircle, and a row of adventure vehicles are parked to the left. A firepit sits at the center, and when I'm in the proper spot, I throw the truck in park to take it all in.

Four women sit in the sun in long lounger-style camp chairs, watching the three kids throw plastic axes at a red, white, and blue gameboard. I recognize one as Jack's wife, Jennifer, and two of the others came to the shop with Lane yesterday. An older man stands by the cooler to the side of a folding table and grill. Even with them all out and about, the campsite appears clean.

"How do we want to approach this?" I ask, recalculating my strategy. I knew it would be more than Jack, but this was a family. There were genuine human smiles and homey touches even way out here.

"I don't know."

"Figure it out as we go?"

I reach out and squeeze her hand. Whether she wants to admit it or not, we're a team. We're in this together.

"Sounds like a plan."

She pulls her hand from mine and slides out of her seat. The door closes rather loudly, and I realize soon she did that on purpose. Tiny heads spin toward her, and Wyatt's youngest son races in her direction. She meets him with a hug as I'm climbing out of the truck.

Being here feels foreign. The fresh mountain air lacks the normal tinge of city smog, and it's just another thing I'm not used to.

"You came," Colter says, bouncing in a pair of tiny cowboy boots. I don't receive the same warm welcome as I close the truck door. Instead, Jack calls me over to help me get unhooked from the truck. We work in silence, but I keep my ears toward Hunter, worried about the both of us fitting in.

While she makes herself at home, immediately befriending The Collisters, I go over my game plan. With the paperwork officially taken care of, I was ready to take on the mountain with Hunter by my side. We would find some deer. I'd make a good shot, and then...*Boom!* Collister account, secured.

Jack's voice calls me back to the moment, "You shouldn't mess around with Hunter if you're going back to your city penthouse and skyscrapin' office. She'll never leave the creek."

Part of me wants to tell him the truth that there's nothing going on between Hunter and me outside of a monetary arrangement that benefits us both. The rest of me knows what Hunter and I agreed to. I hear that musical laugh beyond the trailer, and my eyes wandered back to her. She was already doing her job, and she didn't even know it. She fit in here. I had to look competent, and she made that easy. Careful consideration leads me to admit one truth.

"There's something about her."

Jack sighs, and I wonder how many dopes he's warned away from his seasonal friend.

"Listen," The truck rebounds as the trailer comes off the ball, "The two of you are adults, and she'd hate that I said anything to you about it, but that girl over there ain't the summer fling type. She's the fallin'-in-love and broken-heart type. I've seen it before, and I won't see it again. We clear?"

"Clear," I agree, knowing that falling in love wasn't in the cards for either of us. I may like the pretty blonde, and faking our arrangement would come easy enough, but I wasn't under any false hopes. Hunter hated me and everything I stood for, and I—well, I knew where I was meant to be, and it wasn't in Podunk Blacktail Creek.

Jack smiles at me.

"Good. Now that that's all sorted let's introduce you to the crew and make up some grub."

CHAPTER EIGHT

HUNTER

I'd met my socialization maximum. The first hour of chatting was fun. I learned the newcomers' names, and the guys eventually joined. Nash brought me a plate with a sandwich as big as my head, a side of chips overflowing atop the bread. Wyatt teased me when I couldn't finish it. The afternoon devolved into an evening of cards, and soon enough, I itched to escape camp. The Collisters didn't hunt on Sundays, anyway. Dismissing myself from the group, I found a trail and started following it.

Over the years, The Collisters and I had become friends. One year, they came to my end-of-summer barbecue. I knew their wives; I loved their kids. But I enjoyed being alone. I *needed* it. To the point where I felt some relief when my family moved away, and I was on my own. I loved them, but I loved being able to hole up on the couch without worrying if Archer would drag her friends home for a sleepover or if my mom's traveling nurse would be by to check her vitals. Now, all my social interaction was scheduled and minimal. Joe came over on Sunday nights. I shopped on Wednesday mornings and chatted with Miss Mabel. The shop hours were easily managed, and they allowed me plenty of time to recover. Here? At this camp? Overwhelm drowned me.

As I walked, the sounds of camp faded further down the trail, and I felt the pressure lift. The sun would be setting soon, but for now, birds still chirped, and climbing critters zoomed from one tree to another. My exhaustion ebbed. The space I stole gave me room to think.

Packing for camp, I felt like I'd made an expensive mistake. I ran through every reason my impulsiveness would bite me in the behind. Then, we got here, and I could tell Jack warned him off, and guilt sprung up like a weed inside me. The Collisters protected their own, and while Nash remained on the outside, I wasn't—which only made me feel worse for deceiving them.

Then, there were thoughts of said City Boy. He surprised me today. He was a natural at pulling a trailer, never feeling pressured to speed beyond his comfort or take a turn too fast. While Jack and Wyatt razzed him constantly, he took it with a smile and quipped back easily. The calculative aura he usually sported fell away as the day wore on. He suddenly became real in my eyes. He wasn't just a walking bank account with a chip on his shoulder, but a man. One who was great at cards and surprisingly good with kids.

He quickly replaced me in Colter's eyes earlier in the day when the little rascal hit us both with a water blaster. While I gasped with shock, he spun toward the kid. For half a second, I thought he'd yell at him, but instead, he sprinted for a gun fifteen feet away and joined their water-gun war. All three kids ganged up on him, but he didn't fold until his shirt soaked him to the bone, and he looked like he'd wet himself.

When I looked for my own water gun in that mess, he gave me a single head shake and winked. He'd done it to take the heat off me like he knew I couldn't be fun Hunter all the time.

This afternoon with Nash left me confused.

Was he the stuffy suit? The guy I'd originally clocked as Senior Entitlement Executive? Or was he the version of himself I'd seen today? Attentive, personable, winning the only wet t-shirt contest I'd ever been to? Shaking my head, I dislodge him from my mind with a reminder that it's too early to tell. Only time on this mountain would show me who he truly was.

Having walked away all the bad feelings, I turned back toward the camp, surprised when I walked right into Nash. My nose bounced off his chest, and his hands wrapped around my arms to steady me.

"Have you been following me?" I blurted.

His lips tilted up in a smirk, and my brows pinched. How long had he been behind me? Usually, I prided myself on being aware of my surroundings. Standing here in the woods, I glanced around. The sky had darkened significantly, and the sounds of animals had died down in lieu of the singing of birds. The sound of the creek faded, which meant I'd headed north of camp, but I don't remember following a curve in the path.

"Since about five minutes after you disappeared. Mrs. Collister got worried about you. They sent me after you. I called your name twice."

The news that I'd been walking around the woods in a daze made my skin crawl. Any number of things could have happened, and for what? So I could dissect the thoughts in my mind? I was smarter than that. The fact that Nash had been here the whole time while I pulled him apart in my head doubled my discomfort.

"Why didn't you tap me or something?"

"Because putting my hands on a girl who barely knows me when we're alone in the forest is such a good idea," He jokes. "I've seen the bear vs. man discussion. I have no desire to be scarier than a bear."

I had no idea what he was talking about. There was no world in which Bones was scarier than a bear, but I let it slide.

Sticking his hands in his pockets, he nods back toward camp, "Should we head back?"

"Yeah," I sigh, falling into step beside him. For a moment, we're both quiet in contemplation, but that never lasts around him.

"Why did you disappear, anyway?"

How did I explain the way people overwhelmed me to a near stranger? Whenever I tried, people got upset. They twisted my words into some internalized understanding that they were the reason I didn't want to be around them when that strictly wasn't the truth. My experience was more like an inability to be open around so many people. Their energy and love would be so full that it drowned out my own until it snuffed out completely. To avoid that, I'd wait until my flame got low and then take some time alone to nurture it back to health.

"Needed some time to think."

"About?"

I haven't known Nash long, but he's persistent, and he never lets it lie.

"Life, the world, nothingness." It's not a serious answer, but he doesn't deserve one.

"Sounds existential."

"More like nihilistic."

"Only without hope, but you have plenty of that. Right?"

How did I explain that all my hope was used up? Glancing up at him, I see the tension in him. He needs me to have hope for his success. He wants me to be confident going onto that mountain in the morning. I put my own overthinking away and smile.

"For you getting a deer?"

His shoulder bumps against mine gently. The crunch of the trail is steady beneath us. "Obviously."

The flush on his cheeks warms my spirit. For a man who commands a room, he needs a surprising amount of reassurance, by which I mean any at all.

"Helping you hunt is probably the only thing I'm not worried about. So, you can rest easy."

"What about you? Will you rest easy? I need your best, you know."

I play it off again. "I always rest easy under the cover of stars."

He doesn't let me off the hook.

"Is that right?"

A new tactic emerges. I walk in silence, avoiding his eyes, which burn into the side of my face. I've noticed that about him. He likes to stare to be an imposition. Nash likes you to know he has expectations of you. I bet that's why Jack considered his firm at all, even after finding out no one in the room had killed their own dinner. That's right. I knew the story now.

Instead of lying to him more, I pay attention to our surroundings. Daytime animals are bedding down for the night, while the nocturnal ones start to wake. An owl's hoot rings out through the forest as the sky turns a dusty blue color. The air chills against my skin. I'd stripped out of my long-sleeve camo when Colter sprayed me down and left it on the bench back at camp. So, I only wore a black tank top. A shiver runs down my arms, and I wish for the sleeves again.

"Cold?"

More like too dialed in. There wasn't a sensation I couldn't feel right now. The breeze on the back of my neck, the heat of his body beside me, the texture of the dirt under my boots. Soon enough, the sounds of camp came and the smell of dinner. My stomach growled.

"And hungry," Nash says. Not a question this time. He learned quick.

As camp comes into view, I stop. Nash stops with me. The clearing looked different at night, with shadows of trees surrounding the lanterns and a glowing scarlet fire. Stars began to peek out from the sky. The smell of dutch oven potatoes were hard to resist, but I needed a second more.

His hand came to mine, and I wondered if they could see it. Did The Collisters know it was a ruse? I swallow down a hard lump in my throat before spitting out, "I was thinking about how bad I am at peopleing. I ran off to get away from it."

"The peopleing?"

One edge of his mouth tips up in a grin, and I want to smack it off his face. With a groan, I huff, "Yes. Peopleing. It's draining, and I don't do it often, and The Collisters are so dang nice that it feels extra hard because I'm bound to mess it up."

"Mess up the peopleing?"

"How do you make enough money to pay me ten grand when you can't understand the words coming out of my mouth? We already established that I suck at the peopleing."

He hushes me, pulling me off to the side of the trail, but his smirk doesn't fall. Fall, you pretentious jerk. If anything, he smiles wider.

"You people fine at your shop. I saw you."

"Joe isn't people. Joe is Joe."

He sighs. "You people-ed fine with me."

"No. I didn't. And we both know it."

"You're peopleing with me right now."

"And it's exhausting. Hiding my light under a bushel. Taking the heat out of me. You know?" But even as I said the words, they fell flat. Explaining peopleing to him didn't wear me out, it excited me. Our back-and-forth lit me up, and all the tiredness I'd felt before my walk dissipated. The person I was when alone came back with a vengeance.

Maybe he doesn't catch the lie, or maybe he just doesn't point it out. But he says, "Well, stick close to me, and I'll do the peopleing for the both of us."

"Promise?"

"Promise."

I held out my pinky, and he hooked his with mine. Whether or not I wanted it before, we were a team in this. Nash had my back.

CHAPTER NINE

NASH

Hunter wakes me before the sun the next morning. Her boots clomp up the trailer steps, and the door swings open wide; she hums a tune as she starts my coffee maker. She refused to sleep in here with me, even on the couch, because she says, and I quote, "The only way to camp is under the stars." She starts flicking on every light, including the one in my room and I groan, burying my head in my pillow. There are a lot of things wrong with it all, starting with my hatred of mornings and ending with the joy she finds in my misery.

The only thing I don't hate is when she whispers, "Wake up, sleepyhead, coffee's waitin'."

When I emerge from my shoebox room, I'm dressed like her. Camo pants, camo tee, camo jacket, and a hat with a bright orange bill. She's already got a smile and her boots on while I remain incoherent.

She slides a mug across the trailer to me, and I notice she's done me the favor of adding sugar and creamer as I take my first sip. The rich hazelnut sweetness cuts through the bitter brew, and I groan with pleasure. Today was the day. Today, I learned to hunt. I started proving I could kill my own dinner.

Hunter walks me through the plan on the mountain. She explains that we would ride up to the peak with one of The Collisters in a side by side. Everyone would break into groups of two, and she ensured we would be together. Then, we would 'still hunt,' which, despite its name, required a lot of hiking up and down through the mountain terrain. She had a strategy to teach me to track the well-worn game trails. Since the area was newer to her, and she liked to hunt south, she warned me of patience. By the time we finished talking, any notions I had about killing a deer today were gone.

The Collisters loaded gear into their UTVs when we exited the trailer together. Wyatt claimed Hunter since Colter wanted her to ride with them, and I packed in with Jack and his father. I hid my surprise about Mr. Collister senior's desire to hunt but couldn't when I saw Lane's wife tucked in beside him. As I opened my mouth to ask her if she would be hunting with us, Hunter cut me off.

She walked to the other girl, fist-bumped her like an old friend, and said, "It will be nice to have another girl on the mountain. Someone to break up all the testosterone."

The brunette smiles up at her, "I'm used to it."

"Agriculture?"

"Construction. Though, I'm on-site a lot less nowadays. This one says I'm going soft," She jokes, pointing to Lane Wright.

Hunter's eyes meet mine over her head, and I wink, giving her a single thumbs up. Her eyes search mine, and I hope she can tell that I believe she peopled real good. Instead, she rolls her eyes.

Jack calls, "Let's get this show on the road, team."

The UTVs roared to life, and I found my seat beside Jack. As we tore up the mountain at a concerning speed, I realized this wasn't an opportunity to get to know him better. The icy air cut through my jacket with ease, chilling my skin. The roar of the machines made it impossible to chat, but I didn't say a thing. Jack didn't need the distraction as he tore around tight, uneven corners. Near the top of the mountain, part of the trail sheared off, disappearing into a cliff, while the other was a wall of rock.

Despite my discomfort, Jack Sr. yelled over the wind to talk with his son. They discussed their plans for the day, where they wanted to hike.

"How about down in that ravine, son?"

"You always hate getting out of it." The older man's grumbling was lost to the wind, but Jack didn't mind. He threw out an alternative, and they came together on their strategy for the day.

"You ready for your first hunt?" Jack Sr. asks right next to my ear. His smoke and coffee breath washed away with the breeze as I nodded my assent.

"Ready as I'm going to be."

Truly, I had no choice but to be ready. I would win The Collister account because I was the best man for the job, and Carters never failed.

"Plan to stick close to Hunter. She's got the best luck." Jack Jr., my future client, adds.

"I intend to."

Before anyone could say more, a clearing opened up at the top of the ridge, and the UTVs fell into a parking line to the side of the trail. A set of dirt bikes leaned on kickstands beside two other hunters further into the clearing, but it was otherwise quiet. Everyone awaited the minute they could begin hunting, a half hour before sunrise. Our little crew huddled in a circle.

"Meet back here around noon for lunch. We're on the mountain all day, so I hope you packed good snacks." Jack explains.

A glance at Hunter confirmed she had us handled. We all agreed to meet back here, and then off we went.

Four hours in, and we were lost. Hunter promised me she knew exactly where we were, but she continued to hum under her breath like she needed soothing. The moment I opened my mouth to ask a question, she'd hush me, saying I would scare off the animals as if she was being quiet.

Regardless of her irritable silence, I couldn't say I wasn't learning. In the last four hours, I'd learned what deer scat looked like and that she and I both lacked patience.

"It's okay to admit we're turned around," I whisper-shout, hoping my words will reach her a few yards ahead. The early signs of hunger began, and daydreams of a fast-food burger with a side of hot, salty fries assaulted me.

"We're not turned around," She replies at a similar volume.

We'd been hiking nice and slow for hours. I'd stripped out of my jacket as soon as the sun rose all the way, and sweat dripped down my spine. When I told my trainer I'd be hunting, he told me it would be important to go on walks. I should have listened.

"Then where are we?"

"Heading toward the ridge." Her answer hadn't changed. We must be close because we've been heading 'toward the ridge' for over an hour.

"We could always—"

A twig snaps loudly; birds scatter as she spins toward me, "If you suggest whistling for help again, I will quit. We will go back to camp, and I will steal your stupid Uhaul truck and go home."

"A break, then? You seem stressed," *for someone who isn't lost.*

"Fine."

We sit together on a fallen log, looking downhill. Relief rushes through me. Muscles loosen, my breath deepens. When I'm not panting for breath, it's nice out here.

Hunter offers me the water spout of her fancy pouch and I take it, gulping the cool liquid down with gratitude. The hydration soothes the flush of my skin. From one of my pockets, I offer her a protein bar. She tears the package away and eats it in three bites. *Hot.*

Still chewing, she says, "It's nice out here, huh?"

I bit back my smile. Hunter liked to state her opinion, then add a 'huh' simply so she could garner some agreement. She did it last night when I stood by her hammock and pleaded with her to sleep in the safety of the trailer with me. Instead of arguing, she told me to look at the stars. *"Pretty, huh?"* She'd said. My agreement solidified her opinion on the sleeping arrangement and back inside I went.

"Pretty great," I agreed, with full knowledge of where she planned to go with it.

"Then spending a few extra minutes in it so I can scope out the area shouldn't be a big deal, huh?"

Two in a row. The smile I'd tried to hide before broke free. I might try her tactic in the boardroom.

"No. I don't think it should."

"I guess I'm just confused then about why you think we're lost."

Hunter's censure challenges me, and I love a good challenge. Instead of replying right away, I take a bite of my own protein bar and think.

"So, to be clear, not lost?"

She stands from her place on the log, brushing off her pants. Even standing, she's barely a head taller than me. Those blue eyes narrow on me and her reply is as icy as the color, "You're about to be when I leave you out here on your own."

"Now, that wouldn't be very professional of my outfitter. You're supposed to keep me safe, right?"

Her lips curl back, and I prepare for whatever remark she's about to spit when Wyatt emerges from the woods with a friendly grin and a woo-wee.

"Look what we got here," he says. Hunter freezes: her words stick to the edge of her tongue as she considers fighting with me anyway. Then, Colter, Wyatt's son, comes hustling around the corner with a smile. He immediately calls Hunter's name, and the irritation slips from her face. She smiles, turning toward the young boy and catching him in a hug.

"We saw some deer at the bottom of the hill, but we couldn't get close enough to take a shot," The little boy explains with enthusiasm.

"You actually saw something?" I can't hide the incredulity from my voice because, despite the supposed luck Hunter possesses, all we'd seen was piles of pebbled crap.

Hunter's head snaps back to me, and that stunning glare returns. She's adorable when she's angry. It makes me want to irritate her further.

"Just a little spike and a mama," Wyatt explains. "Nothing worth following."

I would be happy with a spike. I didn't need a trophy, just dinner. The deer could still be green, and I would be happy as long as it was dead. The bigger the antlers, the more impressive I might be to The Collisters, but I knew any kill would meet the mark. I personally cared about how fast I could get it done so I could get back to my normal life. Not that I'd thought about my normal life much since meeting Hunter. I've been too busy trying to figure her out.

"How'd you find your way over here, anyway?" Wyatt asks, and I smirk in her direction.

She rolls her eyes at me, and I can't help but feel like I've won. Nash, one. Hunter, zero.

"Today, we were getting a lay of the land. I can see why you and Colter like this section. Terrain's not as complicated. The trails lead right down into that valley." Hunter says, like maybe we weren't lost. I search for any hint of deception but don't find anything out of the ordinary and begin to second-guess myself.

"Wanna walk back with us for lunch?" Colter asks, and I defer to Hunter. She's my hunting guide, after all.

She nods, going to pick up her pack, but I take it from her. It's the gentlemanly thing to do. Her fists clench, her shoulders reaching her ears like she's angry. I'm exhausted, but the short break helped. Now that we'd been caught seconds from a knock-out, drag-out fight, I wanted to smooth over anything Wyatt and his son might have seen. Her head snaps to mine, and I dare her to fight me with an arched brow and a glance at our audience. Slowly, her fists unclench, her shoulders fall away from her ears, and she sighs. I smile as a hint for her, and she whispers, "Don't push your luck."

"Wouldn't dream of it, love."

Her eyes widen, and I decide I like it. If she's going to call me Bones, a nickname I still don't understand, then I'll call her love. Her reaction to it was delightfully irate.

I can tell she wants to snap back, but she remembers our audience and stomps ahead with Colter instead. Maybe I needed to recalculate our points because as she walked away from me, I remembered her words from before. Hunter told me I was more likely to die on this mountain than kill on it, and without her by my side, that felt suspiciously close to the truth.

CHAPTER TEN

HUNTER

We spend the afternoon lazily hunting the mountain. After lunch, Jack and Wyatt broke off together to go check out a spot neither of their partners could get into while Colter and Jack Sr. played cards under a tree. Lane and his wife said they were off again as soon as they finished their food, and we were close behind them.

As Nash and I walked, I ignored his every word. He tried to start multiple conversations, and I shut every one of them down.

Anger still pulsed through me from this morning. He treated me like I was incompetent at every turn. *We're lost* and then carrying my pack? Who even did that? *He* was the one huffing like a broken smoker all morning. If it weren't for the glimpse of muscle I got during the water fight yesterday, I wouldn't believe he'd exercised a day in his life. Then, he had the audacity to take my pack from me? Insanity.

"Can you slow down?" He gasps. Bones didn't even have my pack now, but misery seeped from his pores beside all the sweat. Serves him right.

"Can you speed up?"

I hear him crumple before I see it. Rolling from his side, he doesn't care as he crushes the contents of his pack. He sprawls out on his back with his arms wide under the shade of a tree. When my eyes meet his, I ignore his dopey smile and the jump of nerves it incites.

"I'll rest right here. Thank you."

"You're being ridiculous," I grumble, stomping over to tug on his arm. He's too grown to act so stupid, but he does it anyway. I tug on his wrist, but he lets it fall to the ground like dead-weight when I release it. Those pretty green eyes close, and I breathe through my nose. Is he serious right now?

When I don't move, he cracks open a single eye, "You could always join me down here."

"In your dreams."

"More like my nightmares," He chuckles, and I kick him (lightly) in the side. "No need to get violent."

Nash curls in on himself a little, flopping an arm over his eyes. He's in the middle of a trail. The straps of his pack curled up awkwardly as he slid down the overstuffed bag. He's not moving, and his breathing slowly comes down.

Irritation and jealousy spark within me. Part of me wants to get this day over with so we can head back to camp and crash like he's trying to do here. There was something rustling in the brush near my hammock all night, and every time it moved, I woke in a panic. The standing part of me would rather he be tired and miserable with me.

"You're not going to bag an animal sleeping on the job."

"You and I both know no deer was dying by my hands today, love."

Ready for my next jab, my teeth snap together instead when he calls me that. He used the pet name earlier in front of Wyatt and Colter, but I assumed that's all it was—a way to convince them we liked one another, that I was up here as a friend, a date, rather than his deal insurance. Double-checking the area, I confirm no one is around, and my head starts to hurt.

"Don't call me that."

"Hmm?"

His eyes are still closed but tilted toward me, and I realize he's using my body to block out the sun. I remove my own pack, feeling the relief as the weight settles on the ground. Crouching beside him, I say, "I'm not your love, so don't call me that."

That same infuriating smile finds its way to his face. "What should I call you then? I've been thinking pretty hard about it. Want to hear the options?"

"No."

"We've got darlin'; that one's got a little country twang. Skull, so together we can be Skull and Bones. Or, for something a little more sweet, I'm thinking Huntybun," He peeks up at me again through a single eye, "See what I did there? Cause your name's Hunter—Huntybun, like honeybun, but you."

"Did you eat something? Pick a mushroom, take a puff off Jack Sr.'s secret blunt?"

He giggles, but in an oddly deep, masculine way. I peel his eyelid up, but those jade-green eyes are clear as day. I tug on his shoulder, trying to pull him up.

Maybe he's not under the influence, but his skin is hot to the touch. Dehydration does some wild things to people.

"Sit up. Have some water," I order, holding out the spout from my pack. He reaches out an arm like he plans to listen but instead wraps it around my shoulders and tugs me down onto his chest. I scramble, attempting to get off him, but he pushes me around until I'm cuddled stiffly against his side.

Like a board with my hands pinned to my side and my head lifted away from his shoulder, I ask, "What are you doing?"

I've never been much of a snuggler. It's one of the things Sam disliked most about me. But even if I was, I wouldn't want to cuddle with this idiot.

"Taking a nap, love," He yawns.

"How do you plan to get any sleep with me irritating the heck out of you?" I asked, scrambling to get out of his hold. This time, he doesn't fight me as I skedaddle out of his arms.

A simple shrug of his shoulders shows me how much he cares, but to send the point home, he adds, "I hope you'll stop irritating me and take a nap, too. Aren't you tired?"

Exhausted. Stressed. Annoyed. Tired was too menial a word to explain how I felt at this moment.

"Well, we can't sleep out here on the game trail. That could attract predators, bears, wolves, and such."

He groans. "Not the bears."

"This is serious, Nash. If we're going to nap, we've got to do it safely. Preferably back at camp."

The more he argued with me, the better a nap sounded, and somehow, with some serious back and forth, we ended up propped under a tree well off the trail with our eyes closed, just *talking*.

"So, why didn't you sleep well?" He asks after a while. We'd covered a bunch of topics, from the foods we craved to our favorite TV shows. Nash full-belly laughed at me when I explained my obsession with Love Island. He said he was more of a History Channel fan, and I was unsurprised. Yet, he kept coming back to this. I let it slip in our negotiations that I didn't sleep well and wanted the nap, and he hadn't let it go. He kept me at ease, and then he'd ask again.

"I can't tell you. If I do, you won't trust me as your hunting guide."

"Too late."

"What? You don't trust me?"

"How can I when you keep secrets from me?" I can tell he's looking at me, even with my eyes closed. I try not to think too hard about the physical sensation of his eyes on me. Instead, I focused on how the sun would set soon and that I had maybe an hour before we needed to head back. Great hunting guide I was.

"We're strangers, you know?" I remind him. I didn't need to tell him about why I struggled to sleep or if I missed my parents. I needed to keep it professional.

"But I don't want to be. Strangers, I mean."

"There's nothing wrong with staying strangers. Even if I told you, one day, you'd look back on this day, and the topic of this conversation would fade away. Your memory of me would be the convenient hunting guide who helped you kill your first animal. I will be a detail-free woman who you spend the summer with. Overshadowed by an animal when talking to your finance bros about how you bagged the Collister account. So, why share the vulnerability?"

I turn toward him, expecting to open my eyes and find him staring at the sky. His eyes locked on mine instead. His lips turn down for the first time since I met him, and disappointment washes over me. His sadness disappoints me.

"Hunter," He says my name like a prayer, "there is no universe in which you are overshadowed by a dead animal or a wealthy account. When I look back on this trip, the only thing I'll remember will be you."

I roll away, staring up through the spiny boughs above me. His words were like an itchy sweater, uncomfortable on my skin and overstimulating. My mind churned on the words, trying to break them down in a way that was digestible. Nash thought I was memorable, and in that moment I was seen.

"I couldn't sleep because there was something in the bushes by my hammock. Every time I closed my eyes, they'd rustle around, and I thought I'd get attacked by a badger or something."

He's quiet. So, I peek over at him, and he's biting back a smile.

"Miss Mountain Woman is scared of a little rustle in the bushes?"

"It's pathetic, I know." I cover my eyes with my arm, hoping he'll leave it alone. Still fresh from the vulnerable moment, I couldn't handle the embarrassment of my admission.

"It's cute."

That surprises me.

"Cute that I couldn't sleep because of the wind or a tiny squirrel family?"

"Cute that you didn't come inside."

"I'm not sleeping in your abomination station."

He sits up, clenching his chest dramatically. "That is a Happy Hauler, I'll have you know."

"There ain't a thing happy about it."

"There's a smiley on the side," He argues.

"A creepy smile."

Without asking him if he was done wasting away the afternoon, I stood. He followed suit, unable to argue with the truth, I'm sure. The small non-nap was enough to rejuvenate me. So, when I put my pack on, the hike ahead didn't feel daunting. Nash made it clear he didn't feel the same way when the weight of his pack had him groaning.

"You realize we're going to wake up tomorrow and do this again, right?"

"Nap under a tree?" He offers, and I roll my eyes.

"Hike, hunt, find an animal so you can close your deal and get off my mountain."

"Your mountain, huh?"

Together, we started walking back up the mountainside, following the trails we'd found before and keeping our eyes peeled. Our voices lowered the further we went until our conversation tapered off entirely. I found that I liked the quiet between us. Like butter on hot toast, our silent moments were pleasant and familiar. Neither of us felt the need to fill it with sweet nothings like jam or honey. We liked our peace the way it was.

The mountain landscape passed by slowly. Deep green pines stretched high above, shedding needles to the undergrowth below, while long grasses reached up to meet the lowest branches. A mushroom as wide as a dinner plate had grown in a colony upon a fallen log beside the path. Interesting wood-like beetles crawled through all the natural debris.

Then, we heard chatting. Colter's little voice carried through the trees and the sound of Jack's laughter met with us. No one filled their tag today, but it didn't matter. As we sped down the mountain, I had a good feeling about tomorrow.

Time to burn the bush. Swinging my legs out of my hammock, I feel my socks instantly cling to the twigs and needles under my feet. Whatever creature is hiding there quiets down as I stomp past. Jack Sr. left a lighter by the grill tonight, and the urge to use it has me swiftly turning toward the creepy trailer. As much as the sleep-deprived version of me wants to start a forest fire, I care too much about my environment.

Since there's no quiet way to slip into a camper trailer, I don't even try to quiet myself. The door slams open and closed, and I hear Nash call out, "Hunter?"

Stomping up toward his bed, I grab the covers and tug, flicking on the light.

"What the hell?" He shouts, turning his face toward his pillow. He looked so peaceful. It pissed me off. Now, he was curled up in nothing but boxers and a t-shirt, with his hairy thighs on full display.

"I need you to sleep outside with me."

Stuffing the extra pillow over his head, he grumps out a muffled "No."

"Then, I quit. Good luck getting down the mountain without your truck."

I'm back toward the door, waiting for him to follow me. He knows he needs me. We didn't even see a deer today, let alone get an opportunity to shoot one. His hand fists in the fabric of his pillow as he rips it off his face. Those enchanting eyes look bleary as he tries to focus on me.

"I didn't agree to sleep outside."

"Nope. You didn't. You agreed my word is law, and I say we sleep under the stars."

"I'm not equipped to sleep outside."

"When you thought we were lost today, you said we'd be fine because you had a cot in your pack."

He'd told me a lot of things he kept in his pack, about half of which I informed him he didn't need. Whoever helped him out at the store really helped him out of his money. Color me surprised; Bones was so wealthy yet so dumb.

"Why don't you sleep in here? The couch folds out."

"The hammock is comfier. Guaranteed. Now, get up. Get outside."

As if realizing this wasn't a practical joke, he followed me outside with a single pillow, and the comforter from his comfy bed slung over his shoulder. Depositing said comforts on my hammock, I help him get his cot put together in silence.

He's angry with me. I can tell from the set of his jaw and his narrowed eyes. Every angle of his face sharpens in the shadows of my lantern, only made worse by his frustration.

"Do you even know what time it is?" He grumbles, bedding down in his cot for the night.

Climbing back into my hammock, I shrug, "Night time."

The unnatural brightness of his watch face lights up the surrounding area before we fall into a deep blue darkness so rich it almost appears black. "Two. It's two in the morning, love."

"Guess we better sleep then."

Too exhausted to argue, he sighs. I lie awake until his breaths even out. My eyes water with every jaw-cracking yawn, but I don't hear the creatures anymore. In their place is the sound of long, even breathing. I follow their lead.

CHAPTER ELEVEN

NASH

We've fallen into a routine by day four. Hunter and I ride up to the mountain together, we head down into the valley and follow the trails for most of the morning, take lunch at the peak or back at base camp, and then spend the evenings expanding out our previous search. Between the two of us, we've had three opportunities to shoot at something, and I've failed every single one. She only failed because she tried to give me the opening, and we missed it.

After lunch, Colter wanted to hunt with Hunter, and Wyatt agreed we could all hunt in a group. So, that's why we were all out together. I stuck close to Hunter while Colter wandered off within sight of his dad.

"Got your bow?" She asks. Excitement bubbles inside me. After my first attempt at a shot on our third or fourth hunt, Hunter decided I needed more practice with the bow. We stayed back on a day when the other women of the camp were heading out to the hot springs, and she gave me some tips. The opportunity to apply them in the field hadn't popped up until now.

Pulling an arrow from the spot on my hip, I knocked it on the string. My arm remained bruised from the first time I used it, but at least the small cuts had crusted over, and today, I wore a brace.

"Down there, between those two trees," She points, and I see the whitetail buck. He's bigger than the spike we saw a few days ago, and he's lined up perfectly. As I draw back my bow, she directs me. While I was much improved, I remained a novice, grateful for such a good teacher.

"Aim a little higher because the hill is deceptive. You want to line yourself up in that spot right where his shoulder has that curve. Then, shoot almost like you want it to go straight over his back."

When the shot is aligned to her standards, she asks if it feels right, and I nod.

"Remember to breathe, and when you're ready, release."

With my exhale, I watch the arrow fly. My breath catches as the arrow skims right underneath him, snapping on the ground and spooking him. I hate sucking at something. *Carters don't fail.* The deer rushes into the woods, and I curse. The urge to snap the rest of my arrows and toss my bow washes over me. So, I set my stuff down and try to let it go.

"Walk it off," Hunter urges, watching me pace back and forth, tugging my hair between my hands.

"I had him. I could feel it." I kick a pinecone into the trees, and a squirrel chitters at me like I'm the problem. Or like it's laughing at me. I flip it the bird.

Instantly, it's like I'm fifteen again, losing a game with my team. In my mind, the loss was my fault, even though I was a freshman on a varsity team, even though I didn't miss the pass. We clearly didn't train hard enough, and I needed the game tape.

I try to replay the shot in my mind. She told me to aim higher than I thought, and I did, but not by enough. It came down to practice. I needed more of it.

"You'll have another shot. Don't beat yourself up."

She says something else, but I can't hear her over the blood pumping in my ears. It was *right there,* and I missed it. I hadn't been that close, ever. She walked me through exactly what to do, and I still missed it.

A hand comes down on my shoulder, and I snap toward Hunter so quickly that she stumbles back.

"Chill out." She demands, hardening her posture until my own 'Intimidation Mode' pales in comparison. Wyatt is standing beside her as she hands me the mouthpiece to her water. I take a sip of cold water from her pouch, and some of the excess energy washes away. Then, she showed me my broken arrow, unscrewing the tip from the shaft. The message is clear. Sharp bit, still good; glorified straw, not good. Hunter's guidance helped me calm down a little more.

"What'd you do, shoot the ground?" Wyatt asks, razzing me.

"Ask Hunter," I reply, not realizing the connotation he would take.

"What? How did you make a shot *that* bad, Hunt?"

Her eyes narrow in my direction, and I plead with her not to out me. She was here to make me look good like I was competent. I could tell that didn't matter. She was about to out me as the idiot who shot the ground *beneath* a deer, and I'd never live it down.

Before I dig further into my head or anyone could speak, we hear a whoop of excitement, and Colter comes sprinting around a tree.

"I got one, Dad! I got one."

Wyatt's eyes widen as he follows his son into the woods, and we fall behind. Sure enough, we round the corner to see the same whitetail downed by a kid less than half my age. That shot I couldn't make?

He executed it flawlessly. Wyatt helps him remove the arrow, and they start making incisions, cleanly pulling out the guts and rolling them down the hill, and all I can do is stare.

There's something about the skill of it, the gore, that makes me want to barf. The two of them worked together like a well-oiled machine, and soon enough, they were carrying the body up the hill with blood staining their fingertips. They hustled past me and Hunter, and I swore the animal's sightless eyes looked at me. It taunted me.

What was I even doing here? Proving to a man that I could be a man? Suddenly, that didn't feel like a good enough reason. I'd never be able to do that. I couldn't even shoot my bow straight, but the kid could take down a buck without supervision. And even if I did, would it change the facts? I liked penthouse apartments and brunch by the water. The Collisters liked this.

Hunter's hand came to rest on my arm, but I was deep in my head. I could hardly feel it, hear her. Her palm cracked across my face, and the sting of her slap was the only thing to snap me out of it. Wyatt and Colter are long gone, leaving the two of us alone in the trees.

The sun shines, and birds sing. The world goes on without me, as it will when I'm done here. What a joke.

"You listening to me?"

I shake my head because I haven't been.

"What was the one rule, Bones?" My eyes lock on hers, and I swear they sparkle like the sun on a clean pool. It's like sunlight floats on the surface of her eyes, and I dive into them to find my response. She asked me a question, and this one I have the answer to.

"Your word is law."

"That's right. My word is law. So, why are you freaking out?"

I had so many answers, and yet none. They were all excuses she'd argue me straight out of. Hunter didn't care if I was out of my depth; she took me on anyway. She didn't worry about the fact that I couldn't shoot a bow to save my life; she simply promised to teach me. I couldn't tell her that I wanted to go home, soak in my jet tub, and listen to Celine Dion through the surround sound stationed throughout my whole apartment. She'd call me a joke, belittle my wealth, and leave me hollowed out inside. So, I didn't say anything.

Breathing in deep, I keep my eyes on hers. They soothe me, even narrowed and shooting at me like arrows. She's angry; I get it. I threw a tantrum like the city boy she thinks I am, then added on a pity party because a kid did better than me.

"You gonna quit?" Her eyes search mine, and I shake my head.

Even though I knew there wasn't a chance in hell I'd succeed, I shook my head. Hunter offered me an out—the only one she'd give me—and I didn't take it. So, while she thought I listened, Hunter started telling me what we would do to make sure I didn't miss the next one, and I agreed to everything she said. I knew then I was the biggest idiot, and I wasn't going to quit.

CHAPTER TWELVE

HUNTER

Saturday morning, I went into town to check up on the shop and pick up a few things to help Nash. Despite his own hopelessness since Colter got his buck, he'd improved. He learned quickly, and now that he was listening to me, we were making progress. We found an area where we saw animals almost every time we went out, and we practiced lining up the shot. He wasn't confident about any of them, so he never took it, but then he'd practice back at camp and manage to hit the target. He was getting better. I knew he could do it.

Walking into the shop, I wasn't surprised to find Joe there, lazing around on the stool with a half-eaten Cow Tale hanging out of his mouth. As the bell dinged, he mutters, "Lemme know if ya need me, but I ain't that helpful."

With my fakest smile and my impression of a Love Island girl, I say, "Like, I really need some things for like killing Bambi."

His eyes popped up to mine and rolled. Joe was used to my antics.

"City Boy become a man?"

"He's already a man, but no. He hasn't managed to kill anything yet."

Since I know where everything is in *my* shop, I start gathering up what I think might help Nash. Joe shouts at me from the stool.

"Why're you helpin' that boy, anyway? The Collisters are good people. They need good people lookin' out for 'em."

I hadn't told Joe about the money, just that I'd be acting as his hunting guide. So, he was right to point out how odd it was.

My guilt over lying to The Collisters was the worst part of the whole arrangement. At one point in the week, Jack made a comment about how he must really like me if I've got him sleeping outside of his fancy trailer. Not to mention the whole *love* thing. With The Collisters or without, Nash had a tendency to call me love, or worse, *his love*. One night after dinner, he pulled out enough s'more stuff to feed an army. Always messy, I got some marshmallow on my nose, and Nash was all, "Come here my love. I'll get that for you." I swear I heard Jack's wife sigh.

I also didn't like that Joe suggested Nash might not be a good guy. Was he an outdoorsman? No, but that didn't mean he wasn't worthy of taking care of The Collisters. I'd seen him do more for them than

Joe has done for me in the last year. I thought he'd carry his moneyman entitlement into hunting, and in some aspects, he did, but I also caught him doing all kinds of things I'd never expected. He helped Colt butcher his deer once it was off the bones. He hung a fly-net for Lane's wife. He cooked dinner, put the kids down to bed, and carried my pack when I tired of it.

So, I may not have wanted to help him in the beginning, but Nash and I found our stride. He was a good man, and he'd take good care of The Collisters. I knew it.

"He deserves their account, Joe. He's really proven himself over this last week."

"Now, don't tell me you're goin' soft on me now?"

I glanced over the top of one of the shelves, glaring in his direction. It would be a cold day in hell before Joe would get away with calling me soft.

"Watch yourself, old man. I'm your only connection to those Cow Tales."

Joe was ridiculously inept with a computer, and even if he could manage to figure it out, getting those Cow Tales delivered took some special planning.

"Didn't your pa teach you to respect your elders?"

"He taught me not to blindly trust authority."

"Well, what in the heck did he do that for? He shoulda beat your behind like mine did. I turned out great." I look Joe up and down. His wiry gray beard and overgrown hair were a mess. He wore a camo jacket over a wife beater and opened a second Cow Tale as he spoke.

"A winner, to be certain," I promised.

Hobbling down from the stool, he came to meet me at the counter, lying his hand over mine.

"You know I'm only teasing. I know you ain't going soft for some Gatsby-lookin' city boy."

I laid my hand over his in return and nodded. Teasing was all part of our relationship. It saddled itself right beside the Sunday dinners and arguing about fish. I'd be with Joe until his dying day.

Ringing me up, I use Nash's card to pay. When I told everyone I was going down to my shop for a few things, Jack told me to take his UTV and card. It felt wrong to pay for goods from my shop for me with his money, but when I told him I couldn't do that, he insisted. He told me I wouldn't be welcome back if I didn't spend his money. I was going to fight him further, but Nash stepped in easily. He told Jack that it wouldn't be right for him to pay for his girlfriend's gear and gave me his card instead. I wanted to argue, but he shook his head. He told me to get anything I needed. So, I did, and I bought him a cold beer as a thank you.

CHAPTER THIRTEEN

NASH

Hunter didn't want me to accompany her into town. Disappointment filled me when she'd said she needed some time alone, and I had to remind myself that we weren't a real couple. It was all a ploy. She was my hunting guide. Nothing more. Nothing less. Unfortunately, without my partner, I couldn't go out with The Collisters either. They promised to come back down to base camp for lunch, but until then, I was all alone with the women.

Which wouldn't be all bad if the woman I wanted to spend time with was here. Flopping onto my sleeping bag on top of my cot, I groaned.

"Lady troubles?" The only other blonde in camp asks. She's pretty, a little less country than Lane and his wife, Luna, and she's here. So, I talk to her.

"That easy to see, huh?" I squeeze my eyes closed tight. I've even started talking like her. *Huh?* Who even does that other than my Hunter?

She'd barely been gone for an hour, and I didn't know when to expect her back. For all I know, she could take the whole dang day with Joe. Maybe she'll bring him home for lunch and make him something special, shoot some cans in the backyard with him, and wait until sundown. I really should have asked her.

"You make it obvious," The other blonde says. I really need to get her name.

"How so?"

"Well, there's always the way you sulk when she's not around."

"I'm not sulking."

She puts her hands on her hips, staring down at me. Meanwhile, I work through my memory of the first-day introductions. Turns out she wasn't there when Jack introduced me to his wife and told me I knew Lane. He simply said that Lane's wife was off with her best friend somewhere.

"Can I sulk with you?"

I want to argue that I'm not sulking, but what do I know? "Sure. Why do you need to sulk?"

"I'm dating an idiot."

Most people date idiots, but I don't say that. Before this experience and becoming stupidly interested in my hunting guide, I thought relationships were for tax purposes. I had my space, my goals, my future, and the women I dated had theirs. Most of the men in my line of work were unhappy in their marriages. Why would I join them?

I ask the obvious question. "What did this idiot do?"

"He proposed."

I look at my newest friend, sat in the dirt. Don't most women want a proposal? Don't they hope for that? The blonde groans.

"You're like him. You're confused about why I wouldn't want to get married. He's all like, 'I thought this is what you wanted, Bree.' And I'm like, 'Forever is a really long time.'"

Lightbulbs go off in my head. Her name is Bree. Then, her words sink in. Forever is a really long time. Unintended feelings for my hunting guide were one thing; acting on said feelings and deluding myself into forever were different. I smack my head on the pillow. If Hunter and I were a thing, I'd be the idiot.

Forever wasn't an option for us. Over our last week together, I knew she loved Blacktail Creek. She didn't leave even when her parents did, and she was adamant that these mountains were her home. In the same way, she reminded me that I didn't belong here. From my improper shoes to my casual clothes, she made it clear that I was too fancy for her home.

Bree was smart to know forever wasn't always an attainable goal. A lifetime might even be a stretch.

"He thought I'd cry and say yes immediately. Did I mention he's an idiot?" She asks, interrupting my thoughts.

"Maybe he's not an idiot. Maybe he's just a romantic."

Romantic notions like forever could be good, right? My grandparents were together to their dying breath. My parents were as happily married as upper-crust types could be. I'd seen success. Just not in my lifestyle. Never when a man had to leave in the middle of the night to sort out client issues or when they were growing into their position as partners.

"Are they different?" She whines, and suddenly, I don't want to talk to Bree anymore. I want Hunter back with her no-nonsense way of communication. She would know what to say to the both of us to draw us out of this funk.

She'd probably be mean about it, though. I could imagine it. Hunter would stomp over in her hunting boots, irritation clear in the flush of her cheeks as she stared down at us. She'd ask us why we were lazing around, and when we explained it was our feelings, she'd scoff. Maybe she would tell me that if

I had time to pine over someone, then I had time to train my bow skills. Or maybe she'd sigh and say love wasn't all it was cracked up to be, so there was no use wasting away thinking about it. No matter what, she'd direct us to get up, get moving, and live our lives.

"We shouldn't think about it anymore," I say decisively, picking myself up from my cot. "We should focus on what we can control. Pick up camp, maybe?"

"You're right," Bree agrees, standing from her position on the ground. "I came here for space, not to ruminate on him the whole time."

That's how the two of us ended up cleaning camp. We brushed off the outdoor rug, restocked the cooler, and chopped and stacked firewood by the pit. By the time we heard the hum of a side-by-side, we sat at the table playing cards and sipping a cold drink. I looked toward the main trail, hoping for Hunter, and she looked toward the mountain.

It was the other hunters, not my Hunter.

As they drove in, there were whoops and hollers. A massive animal, bigger than any deer I'd seen, was piled over the back of the UTV. Blood stained its hide, and a bright orange rope strapped it down.

Lane and Wyatt hopped out of their machines before they were fully stopped, working fast to untie the beast and get him strung into the tree like the first. Unlike the first deer, where they let him hang in the bag overnight, they immediately got to work. Jack and Wyatt worked in tandem to skin the animal right beside camp.

Bree and I were both frozen in shock.

"Feel like you've joined a cult yet?" Bree asks.

"A little."

"You should ask Luna about it. She'll tell you how to cope."

I'm about to ask her what the heck she means by that, but the sound of another UTV comes cruising through, and my eyes fly to the main trail.

Behind the wheel of a machine is the woman I'd hoped to see. She's blasting music, colorful lights flashing as she tears into the camp. Little wisps of golden-blonde hair stray from her braid. Dust spirals all around her as she slides to a stop beside the other machines. I'm already standing to greet her, but Hunter doesn't see me. She's busy taking in the animal hanging from the tree.

"Who took down the elk?" She calls, holding a paper bag and a tall boy in one hand.

Wyatt's grin is enough to answer her question, and she congratulates him, fist-bumping his dirty fingers. They chat back and forth for a while as they work, likely going over where he found it and how it went down. I try to focus on the cards as Bree kicks my trash in the latest round. Then, she walks toward me.

Hunter breaks away from them and her eyes seek me out, and I smile in her direction. Her eyes roll when they find mine locked on her, but she finds her way over to me anyway.

"Camp looks great. Can I assume that's thanks to you?"

"We worked together," Bree answers for us. "Got any sour candy?"

Hunter, always prepared like she is, pulls out a bag of Sour Patch Kids, tossing them in Bree's direction before cracking open the tall boy and handing it to me.

"I'm sure you're an IPA guy, but this is what I had."

I take it from her, sipping down the sour liquid. Beer has never been my favorite, but she got it for me. So, I drink it. From her, it's better than wine or whiskey.

Bree looks between us. While Hunter watches them skin the elk, I'm mesmerized by her. When I look back to Bree, she mouths 'pathetic,' but I don't care. If I could only stare at her for this small blip in time, then I needed to get my fill.

No one went out to hunt that afternoon. With another tag filled, they wanted to finish parting him out before the heat ruined the meat. So, with the men working well into the night, the understanding was that we wouldn't be going out in the morning either. My watch told me it was well after midnight by the time we all went to sleep that night, and it was even later when my dreams turned from pleasant to weird.

In my dream, I was propped up on my couch in an apartment I'd never seen, watching over my girl with honey-blonde hair. Her head was in my lap, and her eyes closed as a movie played on a TV in front of us. I had a feeling she'd slept through half the film, but I wasn't sure. It was some horror movie, and life-sized beetles tore through a city, crawling through buildings like the underbrush of the forest.

When I turned back to the TV, they seemed to scuttle out, infiltrating the room. I had to protect her from them, but they came for my legs. Crawling, writing, biting, I could feel them. Panic overtook me as I batted away these overgrown creatures until I shot awake.

But the writhing was in my sleeping bag, and panic swirled through me. I wasn't in the safety of an apartment, and it wasn't a movie. There was something in my bag with me. There were many somethings. Kicking my legs, fighting with the zipper that appeared to be stuck, I bite back my noises of distress, but the cot squeaks and rattles.

A little chitter sounds from beneath as I try to scramble backward with my feet, and I yip.

"Do you hear that?" Hunter grumbles, her voice finding me in the dark.

"It's in my bag," I whisper back, kicking my leg out roughly as some tiny creature uses my leg as a trail. Right as I was about to flip from my cot and army crawl out of the bag, the zipper came down. Hunter's lantern illuminated our small corner of the forest, and I watched as four little field mice dipped into a half-dozen holes inside the lining of my bag.

Tiny eyes peered out from tunnels of stuffing, dashing between one hole and the next and squeaking at one another to discuss the big, bad human.

"They're so cute," Hunter whispers as my heart tries to slow down.

Glancing up at the sky, I gather myself. Stars stipple the sky in thick streams of light, their individual shades of light spinning and mingling. One glance at my sleeping bag has my skin crawling, and my eyes snap back to the sky.

I focus on finding constellations among the mess. The big dipper, Orion's belt, shapes I'd learned about in secondary school. Every day roughing it gets harder, and the only thing that makes it better is the girl rocking in her hammock next to me, trying not to giggle at my distress.

"This isn't funny," I whisper. Gooseflesh erupts across my skin, and I brush it away as the cool night breeze skims my skin.

"It's a little funny."

My eyes snap to hers, and I can see the mirth swimming in them like the stars in the sky above. The mischievous twinkle there does more to soothe my fast-beating heart than the stars.

"It wasn't funny when you were panicking about them in the bushes."

"That was days ago," She argues, but there's no heat behind her words. Her voice still holds that sleepy rasp I've come to know from our late-night chats.

"No wonder we haven't heard them. They've been moving in."

She giggles at this, and I glare in her direction. She only laughs harder. The sound washes away the rest of my anxiety, and I start to chuckle with her. Soon enough, we're both stifling our laughs, trying to bury them beneath our hands. We're both ridiculous.

"Are you going inside?" She asks when we both catch our breaths.

One look at the trailer has my heart dropping. I'm not sure when the cot went from another discomfort to overcome to the place I'd rather be. Quiet nights in general comfort turned into late-night whispers and sleeping beneath the moon, waking with the sky. The transformation happened without me even knowing it, and now that she gave me the option to go inside, I didn't want it.

In the same way I wanted to look at her every chance I got for the time that I had, I wanted to spend every limited moment with her. Awake or not.

"Eh. They can have the bag. I'll use the blanket."

"You sure?" Hunter asks, her brows knitting together at my decision.

I nodded to avoid over-explaining myself. It was easier to bob my head in agreement than tell her that I wanted things that I could never have with her. Experiences that could only come from getting closer and end in a broken heart.

"Great. Okay. I'll help."

She helped me situate their new home near their bush with the comfort and warmth of zero-degree fill. Then, in a hoodie and my comforter, we fell back to sleep.

CHAPTER FOURTEEN

HUNTER

"Good morning, party people!" Calls a voice even my subconscious recognizes as dangerous. Peeking over the edge of my hammock, I see Sam. His arms are up like we're in the crowd at one of his rides, but his long hair is pulled back neatly. He's grinnin' like he won the circuit, and he's dressed like he's here to hunt.

"Who the hell is that? And why is he shouting?" Nash asks, and my eyes dip to him. In the morning sun, he's stripped out of his hoodie, and my eyes lock on the muscles of his arms. Makes no sense for him to have those when all he does at home is paperwork.

"That's Sam," I whisper. "My ex."

Vocalizing it acted as the reminder I needed. I curse.

"That's Sam," I repeat, like an idiot. "My ex." Swinging my legs over the edge of the hammock, I pull my braid down, finger-combing my hair. Leaning down to Nash, I whisper, "Time to act like we're together," and then my lips land on his cheek.

His eyes widen, and he yawns, trying to catch up with me. Rubbing the sleep-crusties from my eyes, I ask, "Do I look okay? No. Wait."

I flip my head, fluffing my hair and pinching my cheeks. Getting vertical, I try again, "Do I look hot?"

"Uh," Nash looks me up and down as if he's never seen a woman before. It makes me feel more alien than hot. I snap in his face.

"Do I look *hot*?"

"You look," He pauses, as if he's looking for the word and hot isn't it. *H-E-double hockey sticks. Spit it out.* "Fantastic."

"Perfect," I brush my hand through his hair and curse the small flash of butterflies in my stomach. His eyes flutter shut as the silky strands slip away from his face. When the sun hits the angles of his face, my heart dips in my chest. Nash's handsomeness would send a weaker woman to her knees. I lean down again, "Get up."

Sauntering away from him, I find my way over to the welcome committee. Colter, who adores me, loves Sam even more. Last time The Collisters and I spent time together, I thought Sam and I would be getting engaged at the end of the summer. They knew him from the circuit, understood his profession, and cheered for him at his rides. They invited him out to hunt before me, and when Sam broke my heart in front of them, I thought it was over. But The Collisters never picked a side. By then, they liked me as much as they liked him.

Just not enough to tell me he was coming up to camp barely a year after our breakup. Cool.

As I prepared myself to greet him alone for the awkward dance between exes, I felt an arm come around my waist. Warm lips pressed against my forehead as Nash swept in, holding out his hand to Sam.

"Who's your friend, love?"

Jack glances between us with an odd look, and I beam up at Nash in a clear indication that *this* is happening between the two of us. Wyatt, incapable of reading the room, claps a hand around Sam's shoulder and says, "This is Samuel McCoy, champion bullrider and a good family friend."

Their embrace devolves into some wrestling until Sam escapes his hold with a good old boy smile in my direction. He practically trips in my direction, righting himself right under my nose until his face is mere inches from mine. His breath smells like mint and tobacco, and I remember for a second that I'm a year behind, thinking he's going to propose to me.

"You look good, Hunt," He says, his voice husky. Nash's arm tightens around my waist, and I'm grateful for the pressure. My eyes are pulled away from those eyes like melty caramel swirled into brownie mix and toward one's like a country pond. Like a clear green spring, they refresh me, even with the sleepiness clinging to them.

"She looks better than good, Samuel."

As his lips dip toward mine, I step away in a panic, twirling toward the hammock.

"Oops! Almost forgot." Grabbing his hoodie from his cot, I slip it on over my sleep shirt and rush back over to join them.

My nightmare unfolds before me as Nash and Sam shake hands. Their hands go white from how tight they grip one another, but Nash doesn't back down from Sam's punishing grip. I can't hear the first few things they say to one another, but from the look Jack's wife gives him, I won't be happy about it. By the time I return, they're stepping away from one another.

Nash turns toward me and takes in his sweatshirt on my body. His eyes feel like branding irons, full of heat as they sweep over me. His arms wrap around my waist, and the sensation feels like panic or excitement, my mind can't tell the difference.

"There's no way you're dating this city boy, Hunt. Set the record straight," Sam half-growls. We'd always joked he was half-bear. He even had the paw of one tattooed across his pec. The two men I stood between couldn't be more different.

I looked at Nash, searching for an answer.

"Go ahead, love. Set the record straight."

Instead of words, I loop an arm around his neck and hop up so my legs circle his waist. My free hand slaps over his mouth so quickly you'd miss it before my lips smack against the back of it. Nash's eyes go wide with confusion before those long lashes flutter closed, and he leans into my act. We kiss long enough, passionate enough, before I pull away, sliding the hand through his hair.

It wasn't even a real kiss, but my legs felt like Jello as I slid down the front of his body. Nash pecks my nose with another kiss, and I turn back to Sam with my signature glare.

"Does that straighten it out for you?"

Every eye in base camp is wide; every jaw has dropped. Sam's jaw ticks, the vein in his forehead bulges, and Wyatt rubs the back of his neck like he's flustered. When everyone finally starts nodding, I nod back.

"Now that we've settled that let's get this elk butchered and get back on the mountain by nightfall. I'm feeling pretty lucky today."

CHAPTER FIFTEEN

NASH

After breakfast, I'm dragged into the woods for a 'hike.' Also known as a debrief. We're barely out of hearing range when Hunter loses her composure. Her eyes, wild with panic, spin toward me.

"He's never going to believe it."

"What's he not going to believe, love?"

I stretch my arms overhead, breathing in the mountain air. The smell of pine is different in the summer. The closest comparison I have is a childhood ski trip in Aspen, but here it's different. The earthy smell seems thicker, less crisp. Dropping my arms, I expect relief but the tension in my body doesn't ease as I take in my hiking partner. Her stress radiates off of her in waves.

"That we're together," She screeches, tangling a hand in her haphazard braid. Her steps stomp further from camp, and I follow along, trying not to smile.

This morning's events settled as a mixed bag. Waking up to bedhead and wild-eyed Hunter left me uncomfortably stiff. Then, some odd pit began in my stomach. The fact that she whispered about her ex barely made it into my mind when I saw her rushing over to greet him with the rest.

The guy, Sam, looked like a douchebag, but our fake arrangement became even faker, and I thanked my lucky stars. I didn't care that I felt like I'd gone three rounds in the ring with a bear. Introducing myself as Hunter's boyfriend earned me a short-tempered threat from her ex and Hunter's legs wrapped around my waist. If the kiss had been real, the whole situation played like a dream. But it wasn't. She'd stage-kissed me.

Now, I wanted a real kiss out of her, and when I wanted something, I worked for it.

"Why wouldn't he believe it?" I ask, needing to know exactly what was in my way. Somewhere between realizing I wanted to be closer to her and waking up this morning, the stars had aligned. Now, I only had to convince Hunter.

"Oh. I don't know. Probably because of my *hatred* of city boys." Her register goes so high her voice breaks on a squeak.

"Hunter, I'm practically country now."

Her eyes look me up and down, tearing me apart. She's got me under her microscope with X-ray vision, but it's just her glare. With a hand propped on her hip, she gestures to my outfit and replies, "Right, because the salmon pink polo shirt screams, 'I'm from the sticks.'"

I glance down at my shirt, holding out my hand to her. Confusion fills her eyes, but she places her hand in mine, and I spin her into my chest. The work starts now. Her breaths were already short and choppy, but I take credit for the hitch in her breath. My words are low as I wrap my arm across her chest, keeping her close.

"I know how to shoot a bow, track a deer, tow a trailer. I've seen the difference between a deer and an elk, learned to start a fire with nothing but a striker and read a compass. I'm as country as I need to be for you, love. Wouldn't you agree?"

She breathes in slowly; I feel her chest rise beneath my forearm, and her fingers cling to it. Her eyes close as she releases the same shaky breath.

"Sam knows me," She whispers, "He broke my heart into a thousand pieces and left me to pick them up. He knows I'm still looking for them all."

Despite the odd ache inside me, I whisper, "Then, we'll show him how I've found them for you."

"This is a terrible idea." She buries her face against my arm and shakes it back and forth. Her muffled words reach my ears, "We're so screwed."

CHAPTER SIXTEEN

HUNTER

Upon arrival in camp, Sam snatches me away from Nash and drags me off toward the practice targets. His bow hangs off his shoulder, and it's clear he was lying in wait for me. I seek out Nash, but he winks in my direction, mouthing, 'You got this,' before disappearing into his trailer. I'm not sure what city boy thought I meant when I told him we're screwed, but there's no way this will help. I hoped my hike with Nash would have been enough to avoid Sam.

Sam hugs me into his side. I'm desperate to detangle from his strong, soothing embrace. When I'm this close, my brain short circuits. All the heartache he caused me disappears like stars winking out of the night sky, leaving only the good memories behind.

For so long, Sam and I were inseparable. He spent the off-season in my cabin, and I was his personal buckle bunny on the tour. I wore his hat, represented his sponsors, and warmed his bed. He celebrated his wins with me, brought me out of my shell, and taught me some of my gun tricks. He knew me inside out, but I only knew his surface. It wasn't until our second Christmas together, when I thought he planned to propose that I learned I didn't know Sam at all.

Despite all our conversations about home and kids and marriage, he wanted the wild life. He wanted me to party my way through it by his side. He didn't understand that I liked my life simple. I didn't understand he wanted more from me. Sam expected me to become bigger than Hunter's Hardware and Blacktail Creek. He never considered that I might actually like it. Never crossed his mind to ask me either.

So, I spent Thanksgiving with my parents. I helped Fischer deep fry a turkey and made cookies with Archer. I giggled with my mom when we were up late one night about how I'd be engaged by New Year's. Nothing happened to convince me otherwise.

Then, on Christmas morning, no ring appeared beneath the tree. For a man who knew me so well, he failed spectacularly with his gift. For his girlfriend of two years, he gave me a mug from one of his sponsors with my name on it. He'd stuffed it with tiny bottles of Jack Daniels and instant coffee packs. I let it slide. Normally, I would open the can of worms and turn it into whoop ass if necessary, but I gave him the benefit of the doubt.

Dinner passed. No ring. The days between Christmas and New Year's passed. No ring. New

Year's Eve came, and the static countdown from the TV played in the background. He swooped down and kissed me, but there was *no ring.* He planned to leave the next morning.

I snapped.

Memories of the argument in my kitchen, the way he called me crazy, bombard me as he pulled the bow from his shoulder in this moment. Split between honey oak cabinets and sprawling pine trees, I remember the sound of my screen door slamming when he left. I threw the mug across the yard after his truck peeled away from the drive. Sam can't even let me live out the memory.

"How you been, Hunt?"

If I weren't pretending to be happily in love with Nash, I'd pull out pettiness and tell him I've been downright crazy. Practically committable. Instead, I smile and put a massive step between the two of us.

"Fantastic," I lie. "Better than ever, honestly."

"That because of you and City Boy?" Sam asks. His arm flexes as he pulls back the string of his bow, and his practice arrow *thunks* against the target near the center point. It's honestly annoying how good of a shot he is.

"His name is Nash. And yes."

Sam scoffs, dropping another arrow into the target. "You're full of shit. There's no way that's real. How'd you even meet him?"

"He came into my shop for a hunting license. We hit it off immediately." As a reminder, we were more likely to hit one another than hit it off.

"You saw his collection of rentals and thought I could date that guy?" He asks, stomping down the shooting lane to grab his arrows from their place.

Good old Sam, seeing right through me.

"Yeah, that definitely set us back."

"So, maybe the money then?"

If I'm honest, the money never even crossed my mind. The fact that Nash tried hunting simply for a multi-billion-dollar account informed a surprisingly small amount of my respect for him. I came to respect him through other things, like the way he never complained about the hiking. If he needed it, he asked for a break. Or how quickly he learned and how all that pride and entitlement he carried fell away in the face of learning. I liked how Nash practiced curiosity about my world. He asked questions and made observations about the things around him.

"Does Nash have a lot of money?" I ask, wondering exactly how much Sam knows about my hunting partner.

"Nash Carter? Of Holden, Bushwick, and Carter Financial Firm? Son of Vincent and Rebecca Carter, Forbes favorite couple?"

"Have you been stalking my boyfriend?" I tease, but he has my curiosity piqued. In all the time we spent on the mountain, Nash didn't talk much about his family or work. I mentioned my mom and siblings and how they moved away. I told him I was named after my dad because they wanted another son. While I opened like a book, Nash kept conversation on the task at hand, and idealistic ideas of the future. When I talked about my past, he asked questions instead of responding with reciprocity. I resolved to ask him more about himself.

Sam's voice is gruff and indignant when he says, "I don't have to stalk him to know he's not your boyfriend."

"Because you're dating him, huh?" I don't give him the chance to oppose me. We all know my huh questions are rhetorical, anyway. "Is that why you're here? Jealous of your ex moving in on your man? Maybe that's why you didn't want to marry me."

I didn't mean to say that last part, and it showed too much. Sam spun toward me, dropping his bow. His mouth drops open, his eyes wide. Before he can say anything, arms slide around my waist and Nash's head comes to rest atop mine.

"He didn't want to marry you because he knew he couldn't be what you needed. You need a man who knows what he wants, love."

I spin in his arms, returning the hug despite my pounding heart. "And I suppose you know what you want?"

A chocolate wave brushes Nash's forehead. His eyes are like spring rivers, like liquid sage. They crash into me.

"I do. Perfectly."

"And that's the Collister account, right?" Sam asks. His jaw ticks as he stares down Nash, but Nash stays smiling. When I look back from Sam, Nash winks at me.

"The account will be nice to have, but I found a much bigger prize."

He leans down, and I know he plans to kiss me. Not a stage kiss either. At the last second, I turn away, feeling his lips land on my cheek. I step out of his arms. Grabbing my own bow, I nock an arrow and ignore the two men glaring at each other. Nash's words appeared more real, nothing like the pretending we did before. They left me spiraling. My arrow snaps right into the center of the target. I don't stop or pause. One after another, I sink five arrows into the target, dotting the center circle like my life depends on it.

My heart thunders in my chest. My mind begs me to over-analyze. My body takes control; arrows shot, arrows collected. Rinse and repeat until Sam offers to collect them for me, and Nash says, "I got it."

"No worries," Sam insists. Both men hustle down the firing lane, ready to fight over who collects my arrows, and my head goes faint. I'm not cut out to lie. As I'm about to set the record straight, I'm saved by a Forest Ranger.

The truck pulls up to camp, and every head turns in his direction. Arrows forgotten, we all gravitate toward the gray-haired man hopping out of the beige truck.

He's got weathered skin and strong shoulders, and I know he's stopped into my shop before. A tiny nametag reads M. Hackworth, and Jack greets him with an outstretched hand.

"Howdy," The ranger says, his voice tipping upward on the end syllable.

"How can we help you?" Jack asks as Nash, Sam, and I join the gathering crew.

"Y'all hunt near the peak, I hear."

"Yes, sir," Wyatt responds, making two words sound like one.

"Then, I gotta warn ya about the bear sighting. A mama black bear and her cubs were spotted. They haven't come down the mountain too far yet, but keep an eye out."

Jack promises we'll be safe out there, and the ranger totters off to tell the other hunters. Nash looks a little wide-eyed, but I hug him to my side and promise we'll be fine. Black bears were scaredy cats. Mamas, though scarier than most, would leave you be as long as their babies were left undisturbed.

Even so, Jack went over safety precautions with everyone, being especially vigilant that Colter and Nash understood how to respond. We all practiced a good "Hey Bear" chant and then agreed we'd be heading out for an evening hunt.

Sam got dragged into something by Wyatt, and Nash spoke with Bree, so I snuck back to my arrows. Pulling them out of the target retained its status as exponentially more difficult than shooting them. So I struggled my way through them until getting stuck on the last one.

Bracing a foot on the target, I manage to pull it out and stumble. Strong hands catch me, and my traitorous heart trills with excitement. I thank my lucky stars it's Nash and not Sam while simultaneously cursing myself for feeling that way.

Sam said a lot of dumb things while we were shooting together, but one point stuck out. I didn't know Nash. Outside of these woods, he was someone I knew nothing about. When he walked into my shop, I decided everything worth knowing about him was spelled out in the way he dressed and the truck he drove. Over the days, he'd proven that false, but there was still too much beneath the surface. I treated him like Sam. Assuming I knew all I needed to, never digging deeper.

And now, my heart fluttered when he stood nearby, and I defended him to an ex. He deserved The Collister's account in my eyes. He deserved me. I shook my head, hoping to dislodge all thoughts of him.

"Be careful," Nash told me as my feet rocked solidly onto the ground once again.

Did he know that his warning had more than one meaning?

CHAPTER SEVENTEEN

NASH

Grown men who are terrified of bears are completely reasonable human beings. Therefore, it's okay for me to be scared of bears. That's my mantra as we prepare for the evening hunt.

After an early dinner, I find my way into my trailer for the gear I'm looking for. I read the instructions on the bear spray before tucking it into the pouch by my waist. Then, I attach the bells. They *tink* together musically, and I grimace. For travel, I'll keep them tucked safely in my pocket.

As I exit, Hunter is at my side. One of her hands comes to rest on the crook of my arm while the other pats its way through her mental checklist. She never forgets anything, so the anxious whispers have my brows furrowing. Until Sam showed up, I'd never seen Hunter ruffled or distracted. She was furious often and argumentative most of the time but never discombobulated like this. I didn't like that Sam had the power to tap her confidence.

I stare at her, but her eyes never make it to mine as she works through her thoughts. By the time we reach the UTVs, she seems to have it together. At the very least, she's not patting her pack chaotically and whispering under her breath anymore.

"Can I drive?" She asks Wyatt, and he agrees.

"Yep. You and City Boy are driving up together. Colter wants us to ride with Sam."

Maybe I imagined it, or maybe she flinched at his name. Either way, she catches the keys Wyatt tosses her way, and we climb into the UTV together. She doesn't wait for the usual line to go. She starts it and tears up the mountain. Our gear bounces in the back and the breeze tears through the interior of the side-by-side.

"Are you okay?" I'm loud enough that she can hear me over the rumble of the engine, but there's no response.

She takes a corner a bit fast, and the chunks of rock fly over the creeping edge. Her chest rises and falls rapidly, and she won't look at me. Around the next corner, the steep grade declines even further into a cliffside. Challenging myself to remain calm, I say again, "Hunter, are you okay?"

The vehicle flies around the corner, and I instinctively reach for the handle above the door. Hunter's speed drops a little and then a lot as she slows to a crawl. She tore off so quickly the others would be minutes behind us, so it didn't matter that she came to a complete stop. We were alone.

"No. I'm not okay!" She punctuates her frustrated words with a scream as her forehead drops against the wheel. Birds disturbed by the noise shoot into the sky. She taps her forehead on the wheel with a groan. "I can't do this anymore. I quit, Nash. I can't be around him all day, all week. I can't keep pretending to like you when he doesn't believe it because I don't blame him. I don't believe it either, despite the way I'm feeling about you."

"And what way is that?" I ask. She meets my eyes for the first time since the ranger found us. They're glassy, but she blinks any potential tears away.

"I'm only saying this because I'm trying to calm down and my mother always told me that it wasn't good to hold on to the crud and you're the only one here to listen."

"Naturally," I tease.

She huffs.

"I like you. Okay? Not in an 'I'm your hunting outfitter' kind of way, and certainly not in a way I should, considering I know nothin' about you."

"You know more about me than most." The genuine admission escapes naturally. I'd shared my fears about this trip with Hunter, shown her how dedicated I am to my job, and proven that I learn fast. In our conversations, she's learned the silly stuff like my favorite color and the kind of music I like. There were things my parents didn't even know about me that she knew. She knew how I liked my coffee and that I had a sweet tooth. Hunter knew I couldn't sleep without humming to myself. She knew it, and she accepted it all.

"Because you've got some kind of lockbox on your past. I'm not even sure you dig into it."

"Maybe with most, but not you. Never with you, love."

She groans again, her forehead colliding with the wheel. I slip my hand between her and her next bonk, cushioning the blow with my palm, and forcing her to sit up.

"Stop doing that."

"I've done this once, and I won't do it again," She murmurs.

"Won't do what again?"

She pulls the vehicle out of park, slowly driving us the rest of the way before she says, "I won't delude myself into falling for a guy who can never be what I need. I did it once and won't do it again."

"Okay. But please don't quit."

The UTV door slams. "I won't."

Her words echo in her silence as we gear up and even after Sam announces he's joining us for the evening hunt. For once, Sam and I are on the same page as we try to get her to talk, but she ignores us both, whispering under her breath as she leads us into the woods.

We stray further than normal, following Hunter blindly. She only breaks our silence to warn us about a rock in the path or to point out a quality trail marker. Despite how Sam and I both push and irritate her in hopes of her snapping back, she doesn't give in. The Hunter I've come to know is gone. In her place, there's an imposter who wears the same head-to-toe camo but doesn't joke and laugh with me.

In the absence of Hunter's words, Sam and I end up chatting. It's not half-bad. We're chatting about our respective jobs when the conversation turns toward the ranger's visit. It's the reminder I needed to pull out my bear bells. Sam snorts a laugh, but I don't let myself feel small. Safety is no laughing matter.

"Are those what I think they are?" Sam asks, and I nod, trekking behind our fearless leader.

"Who is singing like wind chimes?" Hunter asks from in front of us, and both of our heads snap forward. It's like she's the sun, and we're mere planets dragged into her orbit. With her active effort to not fall for me in full effect and my active effort to fall so hard that she came after me, I didn't feel threatened by this other guy. If anything, I understood him. Sam looked at her like he knew he messed up because he did.

"That would be city-slicker."

"Your phone got service up here, Bones? Shut it up." Despite her retort, she doesn't look our way. Her eyes are firmly locked ahead.

"Way better, Hunt. You ought to take a look."

I take three more tinkling steps before she turns to look. Hunter's inspection starts at the top of my head and moves down my body until they land on the row of bells hanging from the strap across my chest. Her brows narrow, and her head tilts, then it's thrown back laughing. When she's finished, her eyes glitter with mirth. The heat in my cheeks is worth it.

"Bear bells? Seriously, Bones? You have to know how ineffective those are. Some experts think they might even be harmful."

I didn't know. They were simply another item I bought in case I needed it, and after the ranger's warning, I thought they'd be of use. Now, I unhooked them from their place on my pack sheepishly.

"What did you think they were going to do?" Sam asks, "Aside from giving the bear something to dance to."

He chuckles at his own joke, but I notice Hunter's not laughing now. Her eyes narrow on Sam when she says, "Give him a break. He's still re-wilding."

Her defense warms my heart, and I tuck the bells away quietly.

Sam laughs her off, preparing to say more when an actual bear stumbles through the woods toward Hunter. She's too busy in her own head to notice. The danger she's in spikes my heart rate as I step away from Sam and stomp toward the beast, calling out, "Hey, bear!"

The bear pauses his awkward approach as if curious about our mismatched group.

Hunter's eyes snap up, and she joins me, spinning toward the little guy and repeating, "Hey, bear."

The bear isn't too big, and I'm looking for his mother. The ranger mentioned a pair of cubs and their mom. This bear was barely bigger than a large dog. So, I bet it was one of the cubs in question. His sibling meanders around a bush a few yards to the left, and Sam stomps in his direction. The three of us speak together as we say, "Hey bear!"

The first bear spooks a little, stumbling backward onto its bum and backward over its head. He looks at us like we offended him, but I repeat the phrase in a deep voice, and the bear cub wanders toward the other. We get big, repeat the words, stomp in their direction, and they find their way back into the forest beyond.

We stare after them, all of us tense, keeping our eyes on the surrounding forest. Sam and Hunter have both put together what I originally thought, that if baby bears were this close, mama wouldn't be far behind. Minutes tick by with us quietly searching the trees.

"We should turn back and head toward the peak." Hunter orders after the threat fades from the air. I nod my agreement, spinning toward the direction we came with purpose and motioning for Hunter to go on ahead. I didn't want her back in the direction the bears came from in case they decided to change their mind about us.

Sam thought we were both being ridiculous, and he made his opinions known as we walked on. He argued that we should move into a different area, that there was plenty of hunting light left. There wasn't. We had already strayed farther than normal, and by the time we reached the peak, despite his arguments, the sun was down. Jack Jr. and Jack Sr. stand by a semi-circle of rumbling machines. Wyatt and Colter are beside them, and Luna curls into Lane's side.

In case it wasn't obvious, Jack says, "We were getting ready to come after you."

Hunter said she needed to share the bear story and decided to ride down with Jack and his father, leaving me and Sam in the same side-by-side. Neither of us got in our own vehicle until she loaded in between Jack and his dad. Leaning over Jack Sr., Hunter placed a kiss on my cheek and told me thank you for today. She remained out of sorts, but I gave her a nod and waved them off down the mountain.

"Good save today," Sam says the moment I get into the UTV. For the first time since the bears, he's not acting like an insufferable ass. He follows our little envoy much more carefully than Hunter did coming up.

"Thanks."

"And I'm glad we were both there today," He adds. "It always freaks me out when Hunter's in danger." His words make me think back to the encounter. Sam got between that second bear and Hunter. She may not like him anymore and may think he broke her heart, but he cared. It made me uncomfortable, even if I felt gratitude for it.

"Has she been in danger with you often?" I ask. He drives along, the dark all around us, making the edge to his side seem more menacing than it does in the daylight. He chuckles, but it doesn't feel genuine.

"It's no surprise Hunter and I have that kind of history, right?"

Sam had a point. Despite Hunter's insistence that she couldn't people, she was no wallflower. She took risks and played her life full out. I admired that about her, but that way of living was sure to get her in trouble sometimes.

"I guess not."

"Does it bother you? Our history?"

It would bother me less if he didn't call it *our* history. I understand that they had it, but he had no right to be an *us* with her anymore. Not that I had that right either, but he didn't need to know that. I planned to work for it.

"As long as it's in the past, it will be fine."

Sam gives me a curt nod. It gave me the feeling that wasn't his intention at all. That scared me more than the bear ever did.

CHAPTER EIGHTEEN

HUNTER

More nights go by. Sam sticks close to Nash and me. Nash and I fake affection. He does this thing where he kisses my forehead like I'm some delicate, precious flower, and my insides melt pathetically every time. He calls me love. He shares more of his life with me. Then, we go to sleep together outside, beneath the stars, and I have the most difficult time not rolling over to stare at him.

Then, there's tonight. We're sitting around a campfire together. Nash and I are curled under the same outdoor blanket. He chats with everyone; I watch the flames.

Colter and the other kids have entered a marshmallow roasting competition, trying their best to provide perfect marshmallows to the judges, otherwise known as the adults. Jack Sr. gives them all ten out of ten, but Wyatt acts like he's at a wine tasting rather than a deceitful s'more competition. He gives them feedback based on marshmallow pull, toasty flavor, and chocolate meltability. The moms stay out of it, cheering from the sidelines and earning roasted marshmallows for their support.

The flicker of red and orange flames dance in front of me as my mind wanders. I miss my parents.

There were dozens of times we camped like this growing up. My siblings and I would collect pinecones for painful wars against our uncles, or we'd make dirt concoctions on the side of the stream. Dad would grill up dinner every night while Mom made some version of a dutch oven dessert. After all of that, we'd beg for s'mores, and they'd be unable to say no. So, we would double down on dessert, and soon enough, hums of appreciation would devolve into camp songs and laughter.

I don't even notice myself at first. My lips vibrate together as I hum my mother's favorite song softly to myself. I'm warm and content, even as the colder fall weather moves in. We're going on our third week of hunting, and aside from Jack's brother Levi coming up to bring kills home, our core group stayed the same. Each day, I felt us get closer to Nash's success. I had a good feeling about the coming week.

I lean my head on Nash's shoulder, humming one song straight into another. The tune warms me from my heart to my toes on its own, but when Nash's chest rumbles beneath my hand and he starts to sing softly, new sensations spring up inside me.

Deep words about finding your way home through the fog of memories and peace of the known join with my humming in the crisp air. It takes me by surprise. Nash keeps singing, and I hum with him.

In eyes as bright as these,

How can anyone feel right?

Ease me toward that place

I might find

You, home for me

Then, suddenly, Luna joins in. Then Sam, then Jack Jr. and Sr., then the rest. The lyrics lift into the night sky like the smoke of the fire as they all sing together. I only see Nash.

Even with fire beneath my feet

I'll come home

where your heart beats.

The place you await me.

My heart bucks like a rowdy bull inside my chest. Nash knew the song. He sang it. In a voice so deep and penetrating, every word sunk into my bones. I never expected him to know the things I did, but he always surprises me.

Now that the singing started, Jack and his father keep it going. Livelier choices go on and on as I stare at a man I thought I knew but severely underestimated.

"How do you know that song?" I whisper, pulling his attention from the fire. I see him at war in his mind, debating the merits of honesty, no doubt. He must settle on honesty because he matches my quiet tone.

"My mother taught it to me. That song is the only thing she kept from her first love before she married my father."

The way he pauses tells me there's more to the story, but he doesn't go on, and I don't push. Instead, we sit together and enjoy the boisterous laughter. Colter drags his mom out of her seat, spinning her in circles as everyone sings. S'mores are forgotten as the night goes on. Then, the music gets softer once again. The kids fall asleep in their father's arms. The fire dies down to embers, and people retire for the night while the chill creeps in. All except Nash and I, who promise to drown out the embers when we're done.

There's a nip in the air that didn't exist before, and for the first time in the season, the creepy camper sounds nice. I'm warm now, curled into his side, but the idea of climbing into a cold sleeping bag and feeling the goosebumps across my warm skin sounds truly terrible. I'd warm back up eventually and sleep as well as before, but I dread that momentary lack of comfort in my near future. I nuzzle further into Nash's side.

He yawns.

"You know, that's the first time you've told me about your mother."

His brows furrow like they usually do when I start a leading conversation. His arms stay around me.

"Is that right?"

I smirk. "Yeah. You've never mentioned her before. Are you close?"

Since my conversation with Sam, I wondered about this. Even though I didn't move with my family to Arizona, I missed them every day. My mom and I had a normal standing video call each week. Dad always popped in to tell me what new Polaroid pictures he'd be sending my way. I always returned the favor, sending him pictures of the shop, the wildlife, and me. Fischer and Archer made a point of visiting twice a year and kept the sibling group chat alive. Being up at base camp had been hard because I missed out on those regular interactions.

"My parents and I know our expectations of one another," He whispers, another yawn stretching his jaw.

"And what are those?"

He smiles, but it doesn't reach his tired eyes. I squeeze my arms around him tighter with his hoodie sleeves curled over my palms, hoping the pressure will push an honest answer out of him.

"Hunter, I know what you're doing."

"It's easier if you give in."

He sighs, "You're probably right."

"So, tell me about them. Tell me about you."

"I'm close with them, but not like The Collisters, and probably not like you and your family. It's not like we all hug and sing songs around the campfire. I grew up learning that Carters win. We exceed expectations. We act with honor. Anything less than that was unacceptable, and I liked my life that way."

I pull the blanket up higher against my sudden chill. It sounds like a lot of pressure for a child, but I stay quiet.

"Anytime I, or my sister, failed in something, my parents pushed us so hard we could never fail again, and that's how they showed their love. I got a C in math class, they flew in the finest math tutor and paid them a fortune to get me up to speed and beyond. Izzy lost her dance competition? By the next week, she had a whole new training regiment and personalized feedback from the judges."

"I didn't know you had a sister."

"We're not close. She hated my parents. Rebelled against them at every opportunity. And since I didn't follow her example, she made my life a living hell."

I could understand being an Izzy in his family. Nash being the golden child makes more sense than peanut butter and jelly, but I would never be able to handle that kind of drive for excellence. I'd fight against it, too.

"But you are close with your parents?"

"How could I not be? Izzy could never understand, but they constantly showed us their love. All my dad's hard work was for us. My mother secured us every opportunity we could want. Being a Carter is a privilege, and unlike my sister, I never want to lose it."

His volume raised from his earlier whispers to forceful speech, but I don't mention it as the reality of his life sinks in for me. I keep my own volume soft and quiet.

"Is that why you want The Collister account? For the privilege of being a Carter?"

"It may have started that way. When I started at my firm, I didn't want it to be about my name. So, I worked harder and figured it out. After my best efforts, it was still about being Nash Carter, and I had to accept that. Now, out here with The Collisters, I want the account because I know I can do it right. Jack needs a guy like me. Someone who can speak his and the partners' language."

I nod, and a worm of approval wiggles its way into my heart. Little crinkles of red still glow hot in the firepit, but the heat doesn't reach past the surrounding stones.

"Do you like it? Your job? The city?"

Nash remains quiet for a long time, and I consider giving him an escape hatch. I'm seconds from laughing off my question and saying, of course, he loves the city because there's no scouts' pepper there. As I open my mouth, he interrupts me.

"I'm realizing I'm sheltered. I always thought I had all this culture because we vacationed at five-star resorts in dozens of different places and because I went to a private school and later a private university, but money never bought me moments like this.

"So, yes. I love my job and the city, but I never knew there was a future I might love more."

He's looking at me as he says it. Then, I'm leaning in, and we're going to kiss because when he says all that stuff about a possible future, he means me. Except a trailer door swings open, and we snap apart like opposing magnets.

"It's going to freeze tonight. Y'all might want to move into his trailer," Jack interrupts. "And thanks for putting out the fire."

He's gone as fast as he came, but so is the moment. Nash is already standing, moving toward the bucket of water for the fire and drowning it out. As he goes for another bucket from the creek, I stir around the bits of coal and ash with a shovel and wrap the blanket tight around my shoulders.

What was I thinking? How silly can I be?

The crashing sound of a bucket of water lets me know he's back, standing across the firepit from me with shadows on his face. Meeting someone's eyes in the dark is harder than it sounds. He clicks a couple of buttons on an inflatable lantern.

"Do you want to move inside the trailer for the night?"

I nod, my skin prickling at the idea of being in an enclosed space with him. Nothing would happen. We had an early morning hunt and a long day ahead of us.

We worked together to move our things inside. He gave me the bed, but I helped him set up the pull-out. He followed me back to tuck me in like a good fake boyfriend.

I fell asleep promptly with a kiss on the forehead and a "Goodnight, love."

CHAPTER NINETEEN

NASH

Scouring the sour taste of bile off my tongue with my toothbrush doesn't make me feel much better. My stomach still roils with discomfort. It started with the scent of coffee and only got worse with a sip. Stupidly, I tried a piece of bread to settle the nausea and thus the spring cleaning of one's mouth. Worse, I can feel Hunter pacing. Escaping the tiny trailer bathroom, I take two steps before sinking down to put my head between my knees.

"Still nauseous?"

It was bad enough being sick but having witnesses made it worse. My mother constantly complained when my father got sick. He had a tendency to whine, and I inherited that beside my pride. I needed the space to be sick alone. So I could whimper about it in private and avoid the shame of being human.

I nod my head in answer to her question before stopping in my tracks. Another wave of nausea drags me under, and I'm shooting to my feet before I can hear her response. Crashing to the floor by a toilet that doesn't even flush normally, I dry heave.

A knock comes on our trailer door, and I groan.

"Hurry up, sun's comin' quick," Wyatt shouts.

Before she can ask, I grumble, "Go on without me."

"But I'm here for you. Shouldn't you be on the mountain with me?"

Heavy saliva gathers at the back of my mouth and I try to swallow it back without gagging. Another heave of my stomach, and I'm grabbing for the cool rag by the sink, laying it over my neck.

"Rather have you out there than here to pity me, love."

She leans on the doorframe of the bathroom, looking down at me with her brows pinched. Those blue eyes have never looked down at me with such kindness, but right behind it, I can see the pity.

"Are you sure? I could—"

"Hunter, I promise. You're better off hunting."

Her eyes harden to a glare, and she spins on the heel of her boot.

"Whatever you say, Bones."

The trailer door slams closed, and I slide down until I'm lying flat on the floor. Nausea assaults me in waves as I curse myself for leaving her alone with

The Collisters and her ex. Hopefully this bug would pass by tonight, and she would forgive me.

CHAPTER TWENTY

HUNTER

"Where's Nash-Money?" Wyatt asks the moment I exit the trailer alone.

"Bones ain't feeling up for it this morning." I pick up my pack as I go, ignoring the confused looks from our hunting party.

"You're not gonna baby him, like you did me? I thought you liked him."

My teeth clench. I forgot about that. Sam got sick all of once the entire time we were together. He was injured more than he wasn't, but he was never sick until the flu on our six-month anniversary.

"He doesn't want me to." It's practically a whisper, and I ignore the sting in my chest. I cared for people like it was my love language. When mom got sick, I became accustomed to helping her. Helping gave me control over the time spent with her, so I did it willingly.

They all speak at once.

"But, wait—"

"Do you want me to—"

"I'll be your partner today," Sam offers in the fray. I ignore them all.

Before anyone can protest, I climb into the UTV between Lane and Luna. Jack, Wyatt, and Sam all have too many questions right now. I'm not answering them even when they ask.

"Can you drive?" I ask Lane. His eyes dart to his wife's, and she nods. Then, we're gone. When we get to the top of the mountain, I'm sure I won't be able to avoid their questions, but at least the ride gives me time to think.

With every passing day, my feelings for Nash became harder to ignore. He vexed me and inspired me in equal measure. Our conversations charged my social battery, and his ability to play buffer left me supported. On the mountain, he listened and learned better than any other man I've met. He displayed trust in me that I appreciated. Without him, the day was bound to be different in a way I no longer wanted.

Lane cautiously drives up the mountain. I appreciate him taking his time even as his wife urges him to go faster. Both of them glance at me on occasion, but neither asks me any questions. I've learned that about them over these past weeks. The Wrights don't ask unnecessary questions. They prefer to puzzle it out and theorize between themselves.

He parks the UTV seconds before the rest of the guys join us, the rumble of their engines announcing their arrival.

I'm still not ready to face them, but the time has come.

It's Jack Jr., Nash's future client, who pulls me aside. I expected it to be Sam. I have my thoughts about what Jack might say, but I keep them to myself, leaving space to be surprised by his first question.

"Is Nash okay?"

"He's fine. He's getting what he wanted."

Jack scoffs. "I doubt that."

My eyes snap to his, and our hunting party stands in the peripheral, acting nonchalant though we know they're listening to every word.

"What's that supposed to mean?"

Jack's brow creases for a split second before he drags me further from the group. Here's where things get serious, all while Wyatt literally whistles a tune as he looks at the sky.

"You think I didn't know the guy brought you out here to help him hunt? He's not your type, Hunter. A week ago, I'd bet Nash was pissed to be missing out on another opportunity to win my cash, but now I bet he's pissed you're on the mountain with your ex. That's what that means. He's not getting what he wants with you or me."

"You're wrong about one of those. He sent me out here, knowing full well I'd get paired out with Sam. He didn't want me."

Jack rolls his eyes, and for a moment, he looks much younger than he is.

"I ever tell ya about how my wife and I keep our marriage happy?"

"No, what does that have to do w—"

"I messed up. *Bad.* I told her she'd be better off without me, and when she didn't believe me, I took the one thing she trusted me with and used it against her. She left, and I realized right quick how stupid I was. The specifics don't matter so much, but that forgiveness from her set an example for our entire marriage."

"That's got nothing to do with me and Nash," I sigh. *Me and Nash.* Like we're some kind of item. This was all becoming too complicated.

"You've got to forgive him, Hunter. That boy wants you. It's clear as day."

"What if I don't want him?"

"If you don't want him, why are you on the mountain?"

I look anywhere but at Jack. If I look at him, he'll know the answer. He'll see how disappointed I am to be here without that conceited city boy who I've come to know well. Jack will see that I'm not here to get a deer myself, that my goal is to help him succeed.

"We're here to hunt."

"Uh-huh. I see," He brushes a hand over his goatee, readjusting his hat. "If that's what you've gotta tell yourself, Hunter."

Turning on his heel, Jack left me standing there. Next thing I knew, Sam stood at my side with a good feeling about getting a deer today.

My silent steps are steady as I creep around a tree with my bow ready. Down the hill, a spike grazes in the streams of sunlight. Sam is off in another direction, but I don't shout for him. I don't want to scare the deer.

He's not a trophy, but he'd taste good enough. Big enough for eating and ethical harvest, and perfectly aligned for a good shot. The spike is a perfect message to Jack and Nash both. I'm in range, and he's right there. The string of my bow groans as I pull it back. Before I can second-guess, the arrow flies straight into its side.

The spike takes one step, two. Then, he collapses to the forest floor, and a feeling of dread overcomes me. *What have I done?*

I'm here to hunt deer. That's what I told Jack. It's our cover for Nash. That's evolved, sure. To Sam, we're together. To The Collisters, we're friends, but with my deer down...

"Sam!" I shout an edge of panic in my voice. My steps crunch and crash across the underbrush as I haul ass toward the downed animal. I reach for the walkie at my hip, flipping it to the proper channel to crow, "Sam! 30 yards from the ridge, near a fallen tree."

I'm on my knees in front of the still-warm beast by the time I hear him crashing through the brush. He's got his bow by his side, his pack abandoned somewhere behind him.

"Hunter!" He calls as he sprints around the tree. "Are you okay?"

"Down here," I call, rapidly flipping through the thoughts in my head like a moving picture. He meets me on the forest floor, and I shove my bow in his hands.

"You did this."

His lips tighten around the edges as he stares at the cooling deer. Sam seems to think about it, taking credit for the kill, bailing me out of the horrible plan Nash and I concocted. He knows it's wrong, and he's not the type, but I wish for it, anyway. Then, he shakes his head, and my heart drops.

"No. No, Hunter. This is your spike, and it's a damn good one. Perfect for eating, not too tough."

I shove at his shoulder, demanding that he "Take the credit. Tag it for me."

"I can't. It's not right, and even if it was, Jack knows I'm here for trophies. That's why I came out here."

I groan, trying to decide how to move forward. Sam never could choose me. For one wildly selfish moment, I consider leaving the deer here and pretending this never happened. I'd file my tag as filled; then I'd move on. No one would know. I wouldn't have to make any more shots. It's not like Nash would notice. Then, the moment passes, and my instincts take over.

"Fine," I grumble.

With a practiced ease, I gut the animal, letting the innards run down the hill. So much of the weight of an animal leaves with the blood and guts. With Sam's help, it's not terribly hard to bring the dead animal back. We were close to the ridge already.

The whole time we work and move the body, I think. *What am I going to say? How am I going to justify staying? Will Nash even want me to stay after this? How is Nash feeling?*

My concerns go from saving our skin to how he must be doing back at camp. Jack's wife and mother were there with Luna's friend Bree. I'm sure if he needed help, one of them would be happy to do so. Maybe he would let them, just not me. As we maneuver the deer further up the ridge, I realize the one good thing that's come out of this: I'll be back at camp before the afternoon heat hits. I'll get to see Nash.

CHAPTER TWENTY-ONE

NASH

When I wake from my momentary collapse of health, with a clammy rag sticking to my forehead and an arm slung over my eyes to block out the few streaks of light, there's excitement hollering outside. Someone must have secured an animal.

I move slowly to test the waters. After Hunter left, I puked two more times and still felt sick. Around noon, I tried to keep down a few ounces of water, but my stomach revolted some more, and I was left to bemoan by myself.

The worst part of all of it was that I sent her away. Previous to her, I rejected the notion that misery loves company. It wasn't right to drag someone down with you. Then, lying there, feeling half-dead, all I could think about was that look of care on her face. Her concerned look focused on me as I collapsed to the floor this morning. I wanted it back.

Now, my head spun from the lack of water. A single sip from the warm bottle beside me proves the worst of the bug was over, but various other symptoms remain riddled through my body. I might not puke again, but exhaustion weighed me down. I reached for the excitement outside, pushing myself to get out of bed.

I take another sip of warm water as I stumble toward the door. The late afternoon heat clung in the air, mugging up the trailer around me and worsening my churning stomach. With each barefooted step across the warm floor, more and more heat cooked the yuckiness inside me. The trek to the door would reveal more than the cause of excitement but a fresh breeze.

Breathing in the mountain air and stepping down onto the cool metal step, the illness recedes. Until I see what everyone is excited about. The hunting party has returned and at the front of them all, with blood crusting her calloused hands, stands the victor of the morning and the girl at the forefront of my mind.

CHAPTER TWENTY-TWO

HUNTER

Nash looks like shit. His poor, wrinkled shirt sits askew on his body, and his normally tan skin fades to a pasty white. He's not even wearing shoes as he pads out of the trailer, breathing in the fresh air. I ignore the urge to drop my deer in the dirt and force him back inside the trailer where I can take care of him. Hefting the weight of the deer with Sam's help, we string it up instead.

In case hearing Nash's approach wasn't enough, I feel him. He's like the autumn sun on my back, warm and impossible to ignore. He hovers behind me, waiting for an explanation of what I've done. I've been trying to work one out since we left the mountain.

It didn't skip my notice that, with this deer, I had no reason to stay. I could pretend I wanted an elk, and I could pass that off as reasonably as my first excuse, but Jack wouldn't believe me. He would only settle for an admission of truthful proportions. Staying meant admitting a connection existed between Nash and me.

I spin away from the deer and find him standing where I expected. He's staring down at me, bags under glazed eyes.

"Hey," He whispers.

"Hey."

Sam tries to shuffle away quietly, but his boots scrape against the uneven ground, and he trips, cursing too loud to ignore. Our eyes snap to him, and his lips pinch together apologetically.

Nash's eyes don't linger, finding their way back to me in record time. He looks worse than this morning, and I can't tell if it's because of me or his random illness.

"Am I allowed to ask if you're okay?"

"Of course you are."

I grab his hand, feeling the clamminess of his palm and wishing he could feel better. "Are you okay?"

His head sinks toward mine until our foreheads touch. His eyes sink closed, and he whispers, "I'm better now."

I knew what he meant. All my panic about killing the deer on the mountain, having to admit to Jack that this thing between Nash and I grew into something real, the desire to stay here with him and The Collisters fled in his presence. Forgiving him sounded unconscionable earlier. Now, it came easily.

My arms wrap his neck, and his come around my waist, and for a minute everything seems good., So what if I killed my deer? It meant I got to come back to Nash that much sooner.

When we separate, I ask, "How are you feeling?"

"Could be better." He nods before his face goes a little green, and he stops. "I don't know how this happened."

"You look like you need some water."

Nash holds up a dented plastic bottle and un-twirls the cap. Staring down at it, he braces himself before sipping off the top. It's not a lot, and it doesn't help his color, but I accept it. For a second, we stare at each other like we're happy to be reunited. Then, I'm turning him back toward the trailer.

"What are we doing?"

"You need rest."

"Don't you need to deal with your deer?" He asks, his upper body twisting under my hands as I push him toward the trailer door he left open.

My eyes catch on the deer we left in one piece. Sam put a bag over it for now, and with the snow coming, the air held a certain icy quality that would keep it safe for now. I shake my head.

"It will be fine. You won't," I herd him forward. "C'mon. I'll rest with you. Unless you want to be alone still?"

He's up the trailer stairs, two steps ahead of me when I ask. Nash stops on the threshold, spinning toward me with wide, panicked eyes.

"*No*. No. I've been alone all morning. Don't leave me now."

I'm up the steps with my arms around his waist in a moment. His arms close around me.

"I won't," I promise, hoping he knows I'll keep it as long as he will have me.

CHAPTER TWENTY-THREE

HUNTER

"You forgave him." I jump from the whispers of Jack's wife, Jennifer, or Jen to The Collisters. My hand presses against my beating heart as I turn to face her. She's pretty and short like me, but where my hair is long and straight and blonde, hers is short and curly and dark brown.

Nash passed out cold after about an hour of whispered story-telling. He wanted to know how I shot my deer, so I told him, leaving out all the spiteful parts. Nearing sleep, he asked if I planned to leave him now and I stayed silent so long his soft snores came before my answer.

In my opinion, the way I abandoned my deer for him the moment I stepped into camp answered that question for us both, and probably Jack Collister, too.

That's why I snuck outside to get some air. Ambushed by Jen never made it on my agenda.

"He wasn't feeling right."

And apparently, neither do I—making excuses for men? Not my standard approach.

"I meant nothing by it," She motions for me to follow her, and I find my way to one of her fancy zero-g camping recliners. Camp seems quiet even with a few more hours of sun ahead. It's like Jen read my mind because she adds, "No one's here but us. Sam headed back out, took Colter with him. The other kids begged Bree to take them to the hot pools. The girl's a bit of a people pleaser like your man."

I bite back my urge to argue. Nash isn't *my* man, but I imagine how bitter those words would taste and keep them to myself. If anything, Nash belongs to his job, and I belong to Blacktail Creek.

When I say nothing, Jen speaks up again, opting for a normal volume now that we're away from Nash's ugly trailer. "I only tell you all that 'cause you might wanna talk. And because my Jack might be curious when he finally comes down from that mountain."

"Fine. He's easy to forgive," I admit.

"It's because he's handsome, right? I can never stay mad at my Jack. He smiles at me, and I'm a goner."

I think back to Nash's pale face, the stringy wave of hair dropping in front of his forehead despite his wishes. He looked the worst I'd seen him, but I still wanted him. I abandoned my hunting victory to get closer, to care for him. I liked him. His proximity. His face and his words. Looking up at him, my hands resting on his chest, his eyes on mine.

"It was pity." *It wasn't.*

"And pity is the reason you're still here, watching after him?"

I lean back in the recliner, gratefully accepting an outstretched blanket from Jen's hands.

"No."

"Money then?" She asks, and I freeze with my hands fisted in the blanket. There's no way she could know about our deal. If I'm honest, I forgot about our deal. Ten thousand dollars remained an insane amount of money to me, and if it weren't for my plans for it, I'd let it go entirely. Luckily, I don't have to defend myself because Jennifer goes on. A characteristic of her, I predict. "Did he promise you a cut of his deal?"

When my brows furrow, her eyes widen.

"Tell me he's giving you a percentage. He's getting twelve percent. If you help him close this deal, you deserve some of that."

"I'm not here for money," I argue, feeling dishonest. Maybe it started for money, but now the situation was different. Or, at least, I thought it could be. The need to speak with Nash grew as Jen went on. I liked the way she spoke so openly about things, but as she told me the particulars of the deal, they had and the requirements, I tried to extricate myself. Even physically sitting up and preparing to walk away. All the information she told me overstepped boundaries I might still have with Nash. Information regarding the seven-figure deal Nash could secure was for a serious girlfriend or wife, not me.

"Maybe we should talk about something else?" I offer.

"Would you prefer we talk about Sam?"

My heart flip-flops from the mention of him in such close connection to Nash. Where conversations about Nash make my heart thrum with excitement and anxiety, mentions of Sam slow it to a depressed drumbeat. I should probably see a doctor about both, while suggesting we speak of neither.

"Or hunting, fishing, camping?" Anything but them.

"All I ever talk about is hunting, fishing, and camping, girl. Give me something new."

I sigh, "I ain't got nothin' new, aside from the boys I don't want to talk about."

Jennifer glances over at me without turning her head. There's a certain look country mothers give that makes grown men bend to their will; her look is worse. I force myself to mirror her relaxation, even though my body remains tense as a board.

"Often, the things we don't wanna do are the things we need to do most. Ya hear?"

"Yes, ma'am."

She gives me a nod, her eyes flicking back to the overcast sky above us. The calm campsite and quiet groan of breeze through the trees help me gather my courage.

"So, why don't you want to talk about them?"

"It's complicated." Understatement. The guy I liked, maybe more, would get this deal and leave. As far as I knew, our entire arrangement remained business as usual. The guy who broke my heart, maybe worse, walked and talked like a flashbang reminder of every reason it's stupid to fall in love with someone from an entirely different lifestyle. He stunned me.

"We got time," She drawls. "Tell me which one you like, and we'll start with him."

After nearly a month at The Collister base camp and a decade of their family visiting Blacktail Creek, you would think speaking with Lou would be easy. Wrong. No matter how close we became, I'd never be ready for this conversation. So, I did what I did best and dove in despite the risk.

"I like Nash. Enough to call him Nash instead of Bones, defend him to Sam and Jack, and want him to tag an animal so he can win that insane deal you're negotiating with him."

When Jen doesn't say anything, barely sparing a glance at me, it's like a dam bursts.

"He's different from me, but I like it. He's ambitious and determined, and he tries new things fearlessly because he's already calculated the risk. I like that Nash forces me to slow down and think about the risks myself and when he keeps up with me in my wildest moments. I like his name and his eyes and even his goofy city-boy style. Like, anytime he's not wearing camo, I'm gaping at him like a teen for a boy band concert."

"He does wear a white t-shirt well." Jen chuckles.

"Right?" My heart thrums faster than usual like this outpouring of emotion churns blood faster without my mind impeding it. "And he's much less conceited than I originally thought. He shows appreciation for our time here and asks great questions about it, about me. I know him better than before, and the way he acted when I first met him had more to do with his nerves. I'm just terrified because..."

I think I might love him. I barely manage to stop myself from saying it out loud, but that doesn't stop Jennifer from asking.

"Why're you scared, darlin'?"

"Because...well, because he's leaving, and I might like him enough to want him to stay."

"Uh-huh," Her eyes flash to mine; that same hard edge lives in them. She knows I'm lying, but is she going to call me—"That it?"

"What do you want me to say?" My whispered words still sound too loud.

"The truth," Jen states matter-of-factly.

"Do you want me to say I might love him then? That I, like an idiot, fell in love with another guy who ain't right for me?"

Her brows raise, "That the truth?"

I nod, unable to say it again. The words already tumbled around in my mind like granola bits at the bottom of a bag.

"Good. Now tell me about Sam."

"There's nothing to say about Sam. I loved him once, but now he's history. He's not here for me, and he never was when we were together, either."

I can practically hear my mom whisper, "Nash ain't Sam, honey."

Jennifer Collister nods. I'm not sure what incredible, intelligent thoughts ran through her mind, but I'd bet all ten thousand of Nash's payment dollars that she knew the right thing to say right now. She purses her lips as if considering if she should share such life-changing things, but then she speaks.

"So, you gonna tell him, or should I?"

CHAPTER TWENTY-FOUR

NASH

Late summer faded fast into a crisp and icy fall. After a few days with Hunter tending to me and her animal, the time came to return to a snow-dusted mountain. With a couple of practice shots down and the morning hunt out of the way, Hunter's confidence in me tagging out was higher than it had been in days.

"Gun season opens in ten days," She explains, "If we don't get something between now and then, the rules will change. You'll have to shoot something with antlers, and the animals are more used to being hunted. Your options will be more limited as time goes on."

Since that first night sick when I caught her sneaking back into the trailer, she's been a bit jumpy and frenzied. I chalked it up to her wanting to return home now that she's got her deer, but she assured me she delivered it to her freezer while I was out sick.

"Is that why you keep saying I'm getting something this week?" I clarify. My confidence wanes slightly.

"That, and I have a good feeling about it."

Hunter explained a lot this afternoon. Like, no afternoon naps because it's overcast, more chances to see something, and that we were listening for a lot of noise because the elk around here should be loud. Then, she reiterated her statement about a good feeling. I wanted to feel it too.

Unfortunately, I only felt anxious. Conflicting desires to close this deal or spend more time with Hunter left me tense with nerves. Over the last month and a half, a whole new world opened up to me. Instead of my cold city apartment and even harsher boardrooms, I spent hours between the pines and firs, sleeping surrounded by people with softened edges. Aside from the occasional email update, my whole existence of camping and hunting consumed my time, and I worried my return to my old life would lack the previous satisfaction when I returned. I worried that my future was here with Hunter. And with every passing day, that worry deepened.

Despite Hunter's good feeling, we didn't see a single animal for two days straight. Not until today. Quiet and stealthy, Hunter put a little space between us today. She'd been acting weird, but when I questioned her about it, she cited her 'feeling' and disappeared to drive something up my way.

While she broke up brush below, trying to spook up some animals for me, I watched the hill in hopes of seeing something. I didn't expect the massive beast to emerge from the woods, honking and bemoaning my existence there.

"Hunter," I called, pulling my bow.

Like a deer, but much bigger and actually quite different, the elk stared me down. All those nerves I felt earlier in the week culminated at this moment as I drew an arrow. The elk wasn't more than twenty yards away. He was too close for my comfort but within great range for killing. The only thing that could make it better was if the dolt was broadside instead of partially facing me.

"Hunter," I whisper-shouted, but she didn't appear. I couldn't even hear her crunching away in the brush below like before. The elk bayed a long, airy roar and turned slightly toward the woods. With my best shot yet and a boatload of hope, I let the arrow fly.

With the thing so close, I watched the arrow pierce its side. Another whistling sound escaped the thing's throat before it sprinted down the hill.

"Shoot. Hunter!" I shout, following the beast down the hill along its trail of blood. Frothy blood drips onto the forest floor, looking like pinkish bath bubbles. I sling my bow over my shoulder, grappling for the walkie on my pack. My hands shake from the adrenaline, but I manage to hear the beep in my ear. I repeat her name and tell her where I'm heading. I tell her I killed an elk.

Holy crap. I killed an elk. Did I do it right? Fear of failure threatens to swamp me, but the need to finish this pushes me forward on shaky legs. A crackle comes from the walkie-talkie, but I don't hear Hunter's words. I need her here for this. I don't know what I'm doing.

"What?" I say into the walkie-talkie, waiting for her response.

Her voice, crackly and unfinished, comes over the channel, "Follow the blood trail. I'll catch up."

Relief fires through me, burning away most of my nerves. I did the right thing. On this mountain, I've lacked the peace and confidence I felt in the city, but in this moment, it's there. It settles over me like my fogged breath in the air. I did what I came here to do, and I did it myself.

More blood draws me forward, and I watch as the elk collapses. The trees fade away as I enter the clearing surrounding its body. Late morning sun streams down toward me, lighting this break in the trees like a spotlight. The elk lies there, dead, just off-center. It couldn't be bothered to do this perfectly.

The sheer majesty of the moment brings me to my knees beside my animal. I feel small at this moment, awestruck at what I've accomplished. When I accepted the challenge, I never imagined all I would learn and experience. From becoming competent with a bow to learning how to follow game trails, I worked hard to get here. Now that I've made it, the moment feels grand.

"Oh, snap. You did it." Hunter whispers behind me, drawing my attention away. She kneels beside me, rubbing a hand over my shoulder as she takes it in. She catalogs the animal, noting my shot and its size. I hear her whisper, "Color me impressed," and can't help but smile.

"That's perfect," She whispers, staring at me now. Does she see in me what I see in her? Before I can ask, she pulls the head of the creature into my lap and wraps my hands around its antlers. She pats my hand with a quiet, "You've done good."

Then, she takes a tiny Polaroid camera and shoots two pictures. The whole time I'm staring at her. I've often wondered if she knew how incredible she is to be around, to look at. Shaking the photos like a personal fan, she quality checks them both before sliding them into the pocket of her cargo pants.

"A memory," She whispers, an enchanting blush speckling her cheeks. "Are you ready to learn the gruesome part?"

"Can't be worse than watching the skinning at camp."

A light, twinkly laugh escapes her, "You're wrong about that one."

We go on to prove that exact point as she walks me through gutting and deboning it. Hunter's a distraction from the task, explaining the methods of breaking down an animal like a proper outfitter as we go. She watches when I clean out the body cavity and helps me maneuver the beast to get out the blood. I'm not skilled at it, despite having watched the process a time or two, and our hands are both covered in blood by the time we're done.

I'm staring at my hands, feeling the blood start to dry and crust under my nails. Warmth blooms inside me from the accomplishment, and a heavy feeling of reverence weighs me down. If you'd asked me six months ago where I saw myself, I never would have imagined this moment.

I don't see Hunter until she's chest-to-chest with me. Her fingers drip with the blood of the animal as she slowly reaches out to touch my face. Her thumbs brush the blood across my cheeks, and I'm frozen with awe. Her eyes don't stray from mine. Slowly, I draw closer. The blood dries on my skin, a reflection of my moment of importance. Her arms skim past my neck, resting on my shoulders. Only a breath away, she whispers, "It's tradition."

Her eyes fall closed, and my lips land on hers. Our shared experience, the accomplishment, the awe, the reverence, overwhelms my senses in our kiss and at the center of it all is her. She meets my kiss softly at first, as if we're in a dream, while I find every romantic notion to this point falls flat in the face of her. Her arms wrapped tighter around my neck, drawing me closer. I deepen our kiss, and a hum of approval meets my lips. Time seems to stop, and the world fades away, and all those odd, inexplainable pieces of existence fail to matter in that moment. The deal I closed, our difference in lifestyles, and the end of our arrangement all become intangible, amorphous. Because at this moment, I have all I need with her arms around my neck and her lips on mine.

Unfortunately, it's over too soon. The flush of her cheeks fades, her brows narrow, her lips turn down. I can feel her drawing away from me in more ways than one as she steps from my arms. I catch her wrist.

"Hunter," it's a question and a warning.

She shakes off my hold, putting on a beaming smile that doesn't reach her eyes.

"Let's get this bad boy back to camp, Bones."

Why did that feel like an arrow to my chest?

CHAPTER TWENTY-FIVE

HUNTER

Crap. Crap. Crap. Crap. Crap. I'm such an idiot. My lips still tingle from how they pressed against Nash's literal hours ago, and everyone around me seems to know it. Jennifer's brows narrowed in my direction the moment we returned to camp, and the heat of my blush stuck to me like road tar since. Jack spared me a questioning glance when he arrived, but I got lucky. Wyatt, Sam, and Lane all dragged him away to celebrate with Nash for his first kill ever.

Now, all the guys gathered around the grill with tallboys in hand, reliving the hunt with Nash. He tells the story well, dramatizing it like all hunters do.

"I heard him crashing through the bush, and *bam,*" he claps a hand against his thigh, "my arrow hit him before he could even snort in my direction."

"Ten yards," Wyatt shakes his head, "I would have been crapping my pants."

Nash laughs, and I'm hyperaware of it. The rumble of pleasure is different from the one that happened against my lips when our kiss deepened earlier. *Crap. I've got to stop thinkin' about that.* I take another sip of beer, attempting to turn my attention back to the women and their conversation.

I got along with everyone, especially anyone who has been adopted by The Collisters, but I wanted to be with the man across camp. So, the conversation happening around me felt tedious at best.

"I bet our luck is all downhill from here," Jennifer says, "Three deer, two elk. That's about as close to tagged out as we're getting, I'd think."

One of the other women sighs, "At least the freezer's full."

Right. My ear wandered back to the men because I didn't want to think about this. The end of base camp, of hunting. There were too many implications, the worst of which being no more Nash. No more kissi—*Stupid. Dumb. Idiotic.*

"I'm done with the snow," Bree adds. She's layered down in a hoodie and a coat with winter boots on even though this 'snow' she's speaking over didn't even stick to the trail. At the most, you found a patch of it under a tree or clinging to some particularly fluffy moss. With mostly clear skies and an autumn sun, the snow became forgettable. Most of the time, I'd strip out of my jacket after we got moving, and I wasn't even wearing one now.

Luckily, I wasn't the only one who thought so. Her friend, Luna, groans with exasperation.

"You're the one who wanted to come out here, Bree. You said you needed space from Derek, and you wouldn't complain about anything but him."

"Maybe I'm complaining about him right now. He's always so warm, and he's not here to keep me that way. Did you ever think of that?"

As far as I understood, these two were best friends. But from what I see, I'd bet they're more like sisters. Archer and I can't agree on nothing either.

"Now, ladies," Jennifer interrupts before they're too far gone, "Let's not squabble over nonsense. We've all been out here a little longer than we hoped."

Jack's wife gives a very purposeful look at my hunting partner. I pick up what she put down.

"Wait, did you guys stay so he could get an animal?"

"You didn't know?" Bree asks. I look at Jennifer, and the crinkle around her eyes betray her.

Suddenly, I knew The Collisters would have given him a thousand chances to tag something. If I hadn't come up to help him, he still would have succeeded.

They would have made sure of it, even if it meant staying through November and offering to make the shot for him. Nash earned their respect with his offer to try, willingness to show up, and persistence in the face of failure. The animal was only ever the cherry on top, and when Jennifer finally pipes up, she answers all my remaining questions.

"Jack was impressed by him in the meeting. Your boy is a real charmer. The stipulation was more of a formality than a requirement, a way to get out of those meetings without agreeing to anything, but the way Mr. Carter came through left all of Jack's worries behind. We had a deal for him either way, but he's getting the better one now."

The ladies move on while I'm stuck in my own shock. My eyes seek him out, and I wonder if he knows. If he doesn't, should I tell him? Then, I remember the money. He planned to give me ten thousand dollars. There's no way I can take it now when I know he would have earned this victory on his own. I'd rather not have that money between us at all.

I'm deep in my head when he approaches. His arms come around my waist, his chin resting on my head.

"Ladies," He greets.

"Mr. Carter." "Nash." "Bones." We greet in return.

"You know, you never did tell me why that's the nickname you landed on," He spins me to face him, and I gasp. He smells too good. Probably because he hooked up the trailer for a proper shower when we got back, and because he has wealthy guy products. Like, so, so many wealthy guy products. I didn't even know how to use half of them when my turn came around. *What would a cellular renewal cream even be for?* Another reminder about how different our lives are.

"Because you make a lot of bones, money, you know?"

"I've never heard money called bones in my life," He admits.

I gasp, my hand slapping against his chest. *Stupid. Because now I'm thinking about k—no.* "Never? Not even one of the many homeless people I'm sure you overlook, asking you to throw him a bone?"

It came out more judgmental than I expected, and he stepped away. Immediately, I feel wrong. He doesn't let me apologize.

"Should we do this now then?" He crosses his arms over his chest, and my heart drops. Nash hasn't pulled the intimidation bull on me since the early days.

Everyone's eyes are on us, like hot pokers all over my back.

"I didn't mean it that way," I whisper, wishing I could disappear. "I'm sorry."

As if he realizes where we're at, he softens slightly. His tense arm comes around my shoulders, and he says, "Let's take a walk."

Dread pools in my stomach, but I follow him out to the path where we previously agreed to fake whatever we had between us. As the sounds of camp faded, I hoped he agreed it wasn't fake for him either.

CHAPTER TWENTY-SIX

NASH

Neither of us talks the entire walk. We never made any plans. This was meant to be temporary, but I didn't want *that*. Without words, we come to a silent agreement that we will sort this out away from The Collisters. Another time when we don't have to sleep in the same eight by twenty cell later. Meanwhile, we both stew, though I'm not sure what *she* has to stew about. I, on the other hand, have plenty.

For one, I thought we'd gotten over the 'Nash is a walking ATM with entitlement issues' thing. I proved myself. I camped under the stars and learned to kill and gut an animal. I paid my dues and earned Jack's respect. Little did I know, she called me 'money' derogatorily every time she didn't use my name while judging me for the money I had. And somehow, I still didn't have her respect.

We walk in silence, return to the trailer in silence, and go to bed in silence. And we ruminate.

Maybe I deluded myself. Ten thousand dollars could convince anyone to fake interest, especially when threatened by an ex. It's probably why she called me Bones. The nickname was a reminder of all I was and could ever be to her. Meanwhile, I fell further and further in love with a woman who didn't belong in my life. We couldn't be more different if we tried.

I groan into my pillow after tossing and turning, unable to sleep. My mind replays all our interactions, but I can't locate when things changed.

And did they change for her or just me?

The night goes by slowly. Darkness speckled with stars turns into a lightening sky and then into sunrise. I watch it through the tiny crack in the window.

My well-paying job, my fancy penthouse apartment, my new deal all awaited me back home. Mr. and Mrs. Carter would be thrilled to have me back, returned from the mountain with a much bigger catch than an elk; The Collister Account. I'd done everything I ever wanted. Yet, my win lacked all meaning.

We wake up in silence, drink coffee in silence, pack up the trailer in silence. And I continue to ruminate.

If my life wasn't waiting for me, if this wasn't some lucky commercial break from real life, I'd stay. I would beg her to forgive me, see me as something else, and let me stay. If I knew it would work out, I would give it all up for her. Meanwhile, she sleeps like a baby, completely ignorant of the turmoil she's putting me through. Worse, I want her even after she's hurt me.

It's not until we're packed into my rental truck, all our goodbyes said, rolling down a dirt road, that our silence breaks.

"Excited to go home?" she asks, staring out the window. The trees blur past the windows, and I can't help but think about our drive up to base camp together. I wondered what thoughts kept her occupied then as well.

Was I excited to go home? Pre-made dinners delivered to my door, icing my shoulders from all the archery practice, and sleeping in my own bed sounded like heaven. Going back to work in a big metal and glass box, wearing a suit every day, Sunday dinners on video call with my parents sounded like hell. Going home was a mixed bag, and a distraction from what we really needed to talk about.

"Are you?"

She drags her eyes from the window to bore into the side of my face instead. When I chance a glance in her direction, I see the anxious nibble of her lower lip and her dipped brows. Her answer isn't straightforward, either. She throws herself back into her seat, rocking the truck slightly.

"Joe will be happy to have me home."

"Cooking his Sunday dinners for him, I'm sure."

Joe's arrangement with my girlfriend irritates the hell out of me. In the city, someone would consider him a creepy old man, but here, he's like a trusted uncle. Her trusted uncle. I hated to think about him and the deal I still had to settle.

"And selling him his bait and Cow Tales," She defends.

I don't know if I've offended her, but it sounds like it. Hunter huffs, and when I glance over again, her arms cross over her chest. She's closed off to me again. Damn it.

Dividing my attention between the road and her won't do. Instead of responding in kind, I wait until we're onto the poorly paved road and find a place to pull off. We can work this out, but my head needs to be firmly in the game.

A long, winding river curves off the edge of the gravel pullout area. Tall pines climb toward the sky; their younger trees are staggered between them. The truck rolls to a stop, and I slam the thing in park.

"What are you doing?"

"I like you," I respond, ignoring her question. "I like you more than delivered meals and my therapeutic mattress at home."

"Wow. Thanks." Her nose wrinkles and she unclips her seatbelt to turn further away from me, but I don't allow it. My hand circles her wrist, tugging her into my lap. She collapses against my chest, and my free hand tilts her face toward mine.

I kiss one cheek, "I like the way you boss me around because you know better."

I kiss the other, "And I like how you call me Bones, but I like it even more when you say my name."

Her eyes remain hardened against me, but they flutter closed as I bring my mouth to hers. I feel her gasp against my lips, taking advantage of their parting. Her body moves closer to mine, and toned arms circle my neck. We smell like campfire and earth, but she tastes like cinnamon toothpaste and the warmth I've grown used to.

People say their lives flash before them right before near-death experiences, but mine flashed before me in this kiss. Instead of long, lonely nights at an office and career accolades, I see waking up to baby-blue eyes. There's the beep of a coffee maker, and I bring her a cup. Black, because that's how she likes it. On Sundays, she fishes, I read. She wears a simple rubber wedding band because she's scared to lose the one I bought her, and we're talking about— Hunter rips herself away.

Her back slams against the opposite end of the cab. Her chest rises and falls with each erratic breath. I'm not sure I'm breathing.

"We can't. You'll resent me."

Hunter's words feel like a blow. They hurt as bad as one, too, not that I've ever been punched before.

"Hunter—"

"No, don't *Hunter* me. We," she motions between us with a frantic hand, "will never work. You live in a city far, far away from me, and I belong to Blacktail Creek. And I can't leave because I'll only want to come back, and you can't join me because you have a life and obligations, and *this,* this was fake. A way for us to pass the time, to avoid telling The Collisters about the deal, to keep Sam off my back."

The pain that radiates from my chest is unlike anything I've ever felt before. I feel like she's pulling me open and ripping out my insides, gutting me on the mountainside like a trophy deer. I need to make it stop. It's real. I know it is.

"No, Hunter, you can't tell me—"

"I can, and I did." She's barely holding it together. I can see the glassy sheen in her eyes, but her shoulders tense when I reach out, and my hand falls back to my side. Stiff and robotic, she pulls her seatbelt across her chest, clicking it in properly once more. "Now, take me home, Mr. Carter."

It's like the final blow. Not Nash. Not Bones. Mr. Carter, something I normally would joke about. *I'm not Mr. Carter, that's my father. Call me Nash.* But I can't even breathe, let alone joke.

Woodenly, I follow her lead. My seatbelt snaps into the latch, and she flinches. Then, the truck pulls back onto the road. I drive with my eyes latched on the blacktop ahead of me until her shop pops up ahead. Her own truck sits exactly where she left it, the faded red like my final warning.

You should say something. My brain screams, but words fail me as I slide my rental into park once again. Her seatbelt unlatches, and she glances in my direction. Her mouth opens to say something, but she thinks better of it. With a shake of her head, she shoves the truck door open, grabbing her things out of the back.

I watch in a stupor as she tosses it into the bed of her own truck. The thing rumbles to life like her bike did that first night; her brake lights flash, and then she's tearing out of the parking lot and away from me.

One glance at the shop's closed sign across the front door tells me it's Sunday. She wouldn't return today, and neither would anyone else. So, I did what seemed most logical. I wrote her check and slid it through the slot on the front of the door. I left my number and an apology in the memo.

CHAPTER TWENTY-SEVEN

HUNTER

I'm a single step into my home when the smell of roasted red meat and onions hits me. My heartbreak pounds at my chest like a sledgehammer against a brick wall. The tears hold, but only barely, as Joe comes around the corner in my 'Kiss the Cook' apron, holding a wooden spoon. He's smiling, happy to have me back, but it's the last straw.

Sobs break out. I hear the wooden spoon smack against the sunflower-yellow floors, and Joe's knobby limbs come around me in his attempt at a hug. He's not the type to comfort a woman; he always said if he wanted to, he would have stayed married. But, as I sob into his chest, he rubs a soothing hand over my back. Drawing back slightly, he takes in my tear-mottled face.

"Jesus, Hunt, what happened?"

More sobs break out and I shake my head. I can't talk about it. I'm not ready to talk about any of it. Joe doesn't push. He would never. Instead, he draws me over to the old leather couch from my childhood, wrapping me in a blanket my mother made me.

He looks at me like I'm a puzzle to solve before something dawns on him. Joe disappears from the room for what feels like forever, and I try to gather myself while he's gone. When he returns, he's got stewed meat and potatoes on one plate. A massive slice of apple pie with a scoop of ice cream atop it fills another. Two bottles of beer hang between the knuckles of his fingers, and the remote I keep stashed atop the fridge is pinched between his lips.

He spits it into my lap, putting down the plates and beers on my coffee table. It's the kind that lifts into a TV dinner set up, and he lifts it toward my lap. Disappearing again, he returns with his own plate.

"We can watch anything you want, even that garbage vampire show, and I ain't gon' say nothin' about it. But them tears ought to stop. Otherwise, I'll be the one hunting."

A weak laugh cuts through a sob, and I pull my plate into my lap, using the remote to start up my favorite TV show. Joe stayed true to his word, and with my tears at bay and the distraction of sauce-softened potatoes and private school vampires, I could almost forget about the gaping wound in my heart.

"Looks like Prince Charming left a calling card," Joe grumbles, swiping up a slip of paper off the floor by the front door. He came in with me this morning to make sure I was up to speed on the books and act as backup if Mr. Carter decided to wait me out again. He flips the scrap over in his hands, and his eyes widen.

"What is it?" I ask, dropping my things behind the counter before rushing to his side.

I'm not sure what I expected. An apology or love note, maybe? Definitely not the check for ten thousand dollars. I'd told him I couldn't take his money. Didn't I?

Joe and I stare at the scrap of paper like it might come to life and bite us. Neither of us is comfortable holding that much money in our hands at once; we lay it on the counter and stare like it will grow wings.

"What did you do for the man, Hunter?"

"I," I pause. We promised not to tell anyone about our arrangement. But then, I go on because we also promised our relationship would be fake, and my very real broken heart overrode any promises we made. "I told him I'd be his outfitter, his hunting guide. Lord knows he needed the help." Except he didn't. The Collisters would have taken care of him. Jen all but told me so.

Guilt burrows in my gut and I swipe the check off the counter, slamming it under the cash tray in the drawer.

"Ten thousand dollars worth of help? Did you build him a debris shelter, too?"

"I'm not gonna cash it," I grind out, looking anywhere but at the drawer hiding proof of our transaction.

Joe grunts with dissatisfaction. "Now, don't be hasty girl. That's a damn good sum, and you earned that."

"No. I didn't. I wasn't even there when he got his elk. Only after he tracked the blood trail."

"He got an elk?" Joe asks, surprised. When I stare at him with disbelief, he shakes it off. "Right. We don't care what city-slicker did. He's dead to us."

I nod my approval, and Joe walks me through everything that happened in my absence. Mostly, it comes down to an extra fifty dollars in Cow Tales, an uptick in sunscreen sales, and one Joe who expressed his enthusiasm about returning to full-time retirement. He stuck around as I opened up shop, but when Nash didn't come around in the first hour, he cleared his throat across the counter.

"You gonna be alright?"

"I'll be fine," I promise him, plastering on my most convincing smile.

"Alright. Then, I'll get out of your hair."

I roll my eyes, "You're never in my hair, Joe."

He winks back at me, and the bells slam against the door as he swings it open. He's almost gone when he turns back one last time.

"Oh, and Hunter?"

"What's up, Joe?"

I expect him to crack a joke, give me some sage words of advice, or tell me not to ask any questions if reports came about regarding Nash going missing. Instead, he smiles and admits, "You were right about the night crawlers."

A genuine smile lit my face, and I knew that even if it hurt, I made the right decision.

CHAPTER TWENTY-EIGHT

NASH

Staring at myself in the mirror, I try to give myself the same pep talk as usual.

"Slide deck, prepared," I whisper to myself, even though I'm not confident about it. My partner left my calendar stacked with deals he needed me to close for him the moment I got back. Despite the short twenty hours I had to prepare, I remained unprepared for this client. Confidence is ninety percent of the battle, but I didn't have any of that either.

"I'm ready," I whisper, tasting the lie as I say it.

My pep talk falls apart as I realize my next piece talks about my fade. The overgrown fade, bleeding into a bushy beard unlike any I've ever sported before. My barber, who usually squeezed me in because I tipped him a hundred percent every time, was on his honeymoon. So, I did my best with a tin of beard balm and a set of trimmers at home. Furthest from fresh I could get.

Even my suit felt wrong. All the hiking left my hamstrings and calves swollen, and the archery practice made the jacket feel tight. Either I'd have to lose the muscle mass or find a good seamstress to re-tailor my suits.

Meeting my eyes in the mirror, I expected to tell myself 'handsome as always,' but the bags beneath my eyes broadcasted the terrible sleep, or rather lack of it, I'd endured since my first night back. Without the scurrying of a family of mice, the groan of the trailer from my own movements, or Hunter's soft snores, I couldn't get there. I tried to listen to the cars outside my window, to pretend the lights from the cars were stars across the sky, but it didn't work. So, now I looked busted as I headed into another primo-client meeting.

Away from Hunter for a single day, and it appeared off-kilter was my new look.

"You got this," I whisper, pointing at myself in the mirror. Spinning away from the mirror, I crash into the hallway. *Confidence is ninety percent of the battle.* Rolling my shoulders back, I walk around the corner, away from the bathroom, and crash straight into an intern holding not one but two to-go carriers of coffee. An explosion of hot liquid bathes us both, and apologies immediately start falling from his mouth.

"Oh no. Oh my gosh. I'm so sorry." The intern's hands shake as he dabs a napkin on my dripping suit. My shirt looks like the color of crap, and my bare skin is red and raised from the uncomfortable heat. His eyes raise to mine and widen. I don't know if it's because he recognizes me as Mr. Carter, the man with his name on the building, or if he doesn't recognize me because I look like a caveman in a suit with my beard frizzing from the coffee soaking my beard. His babbling gives away the answer. He gasps, "Mr. Carter. I'm so sorry. Please don't fire me."

I look at the conference room ahead of me. My partner held over the clients, offering them all a drink in preparation for me. Making them promises I might not be able to keep.

I look down at the intern. "Get me a suit from the shop two doors down. They have my measurements."

"I'm not fired?"

"Do you want to be? You've made me late to my meeting. Move."

The intern sprints down the hall much faster than before, the coffee forgotten. As another person comes down the hall, I ask them politely, "Can you get someone to clean this up? Thanks."

I wash my face in the sink, stripping out of the soiled shirt. My voice is angry as I force my pep talk out again. I'm ready. Fade looks fresh. Face, handsome as always. I don't believe any of it, even after the intern returns with a new suit in a deep navy color, with a crisp white shirt and emerald accessories. At least the unfinished tailoring fits more comfortably.

My entrance to the conference room stops everyone in their tracks, and I thank them for their patience. When I turn around, my partner's brows crinkle, but I give him the signal that I have this covered. Then, I take them through the worst presentation I've ever given in my life. They stop me at every turn, asking questions I am completely unprepared for or telling me I got certain numbers wrong, so I had to adjust on the fly.

I'm not bad at my job, so I only stumble through a couple slides before ditching my presentation entirely and playing it like a conversation. We get to a point where they can consider us, but when it comes to their packets, none of the information is correct. I promise them updated information, hand-delivered, by end of day. They refuse to put a second meeting on the calendar, and I know I've lost them. My first loss ever.

The door to the conference closes behind them, and my partner whirls on me.

"What in the Sam Hill was that?" His voice raises, but it's soundproof glass. Everyone outside only sees him waving his hands around wildly. "And what happened to your game-day suit?"

"Coffee accident," I explain, ignoring his first question. Somehow, my cares about that client were gone. Who cares if I lose a single account out of my entire career? Not me.

"Something on that mountain changed you, and I need you to change it back," My partner grumbles, glaring down at me. I shrug. He doesn't know there's no going back. I don't want to live like the Nash that came before, the one who didn't know about a blondie named Hunter. He sighs, pinching his nose, "Take the rest of the day to get yourself together. I'll handle your meetings."

When I stand from my chair, numbness curls through me. Carters win, but for the first time, I lost. And I'm not talking about the client.

I don't go home, where all my hunting gear lies in piles across my living room, and packages of elk steaks fill my freezer. Instead, I retreat to my office and throw myself into work. My partner packed my schedule so full, I do my best to tackle presentation by presentation, double-checking my work so I don't fail again. I even send out updated packets to the people I let down.

By the time I'm about to admit defeat, darkness has enveloped the sky, making way for the glow of streetlights below. The automatic lights in the hall have shut off, aside from my assistant's desk. When I work, she works, and she's triple-checking each presentation I've created. So, we're both still here with Thai food from our favorite spot cooling beside us. I prepare to shut down my computer when I hear the *ding* of my email and thank the heavens above. It's from Lane Wright, the finished Collister deal.

As I go to click into it, I hear my assistant shouting in the hall.

"Do you have an appointment?" She screeches like anyone is on my calendar near midnight. I stand from my desk, preparing to intercept the person, but my door flings open seconds before my visitor can burst in. My assistant looks disheveled and blocks the man with her body. "You have a visitor, sir. Joe…"

She glances over her shoulder at the man, waiting for him to supply his last name. I bite back my urge to smile when he doesn't give it. Instead, Joe shoves his way past her. His finger collides with my chest, and he growls, "We had a deal."

"Do you want me to call security?" She asks, glancing between two disheveled men with anxiety.

I look past Joe to shake my head. "Don't worry about it. In fact, why don't you head home for the night?"

"Are you sure, sir? I haven't finished those—"

"They can wait 'til morning."

My assistant needs no more convincing. With a nod and an awkward curtsy, she dips from the room and gathers up her things. The light outside my office flicks off and then it's just me, Joe, and some dues I haven't yet paid.

CHAPTER TWENTY-NINE

HUNTER

Joe's sketchy behavior becomes apparent the next morning while I'm wallowing. My eyes have been affixed to the same spot on the wood beam of my ceiling for hours, sad country music blasting from my record player. A package of original Oreos and tissues are both within reach, but I haven't been able to cry since last night. Then, the front door creaks open. *I've been meaning to hit the hinge with some WD-40.* Ain't doing that right now, though.

"Joe?" I call out, but no answer comes. It takes some effort, but I sit up, grabbing my handgun from my nightstand. "Hello?"

My bad luck could certainly get worse. Broken hearts and break-ins go together just right. Crawling toward the edge of my bed, one-foot lands on the cool wood floor before a familiar voice sings through the house.

"Put the gun down, sweetie. It's Pops and me," My mother says, coming around the corner as I'm setting down the gun. She wastes no time, throwing herself into my outstretched arms, and I squeeze her tight. She's got a pair of readers perched atop her head and a bright smile. She looks good. Healthy.

"What are you doing here?"

My father answers, coming around the corner to join us. He's holding a beer from my fridge and trying to open it with his belt buckle. My mom shucked her shoes off at the front door like old times, but my dad still wears his boots as he clomps over a new rug.

My parents—bless their hearts—try their best to treat the house like mine, but it was theirs first. So, despite the introduction of my handmade pieces and some new decorations, they treated it like their own. Dad's boots on my rug included.

"Old Joe gave us a call, said you were our child and therefore our problem."

I snort. "Good old Joe."

Apparently he couldn't deal with my crying for even one night. No wonder he spent so long in the kitchen.

My mother balks, "He said nothing of the sort."

My dad mouths over her shoulder, 'he did so.'

"Joe told us you were crying. He said some city-boy came through and really did a doozy on you. Oh! And he said you tagged a deer this season."

Dad gives me a big thumbs up over that one, taking a long pull of the beer.

"It was a spike," I explain.

"Better for eatin'."

"Your father's right. Sad to die young, but delicious with a side of funeral potatoes," my mom nods emphatically, and I can't help but laugh. "Now, let's get comfortable. I never did get used to that curvy mountain drive."

She helps me scoot up toward the headboard, and soon enough, we're both leaning against it. The package of Oreos rests in her lap. Dad dips out to return with a beer for each of us, and then he pops out again to return with one of my chairs from the living room. He plops down into it backward, with his elbows resting on the back of the chair.

In the silence, I can tell they want to ask about him, but I'm still not ready to talk about it.

"How's Archer?"

"You can ask her yourself when she gets in tomorrow." Mom pats my hand. "And Fischer, too."

"They're coming back to Blacktail Creek?"

"Yes, baby. They'll be here in the morning."

We sit in the quiet again. My mom holds my hand, keeping her eyes on me, and my dad stares me down, taking another sip of his beer. He's never been one for many words, but I can tell this time, he's holding them back. They want me to open up in my own time, but they're not going to let me distract myself. So, I reach for the Oreos, and Mom snatches them away.

"Details first. Oreos later." Dad says, acting as her backup.

I sigh, crushing one of my pillows into my chest until it poofs like risen dough. Then, I spill it.

Every little detail, from the way Nash treated me when he first rolled into town to the change I saw in him when we got up to camp to how blurry the lines got when Sam showed up, comes tumbling out of my mouth. Even the part about our deal. Mom had a lot to say about Sam, cursing that 'bullheaded bullrider.' She called him a 'wandering gypsy sent to steal my heart,' and my dad nodded like he heard all this before. When she's done dogging on my ex, I tell them that I think I might love him—Nash, not Sam— but he's just like Sam. He'll never settle down for me.

"Is that what he said?" My dad asks from across the room. His tone sounds bored, but that's no different from usual. Hunter Sr. has a dry voice and an even drier sense of humor. It's one of the things I loved about him, probably because I spoke more bubbly like my mom.

I try to recall Nash's exact words, but when I replay our conversation in the truck, all I can remember is the panic inside me. We didn't speak for hours on end, and then he opened it up with something about liking me. He liked me. He didn't love me. And everything that happened afterward, I produced from the need to get out before it got even more serious.

The problem remained beside my hurt. I'm already more serious. He talked about his deep affection for me, and I had to physically restrain myself from saying, 'I love you.' It's possible that the love happened in one of those moments, or maybe gradually from the moment he stepped foot inside my shop.

"Well, did he, sweetie? Say he didn't want to settle down? Wouldn't even consider Blacktail Creek?"

My mom's eyes, a mirror image of mine, peek down at me. There's no judgment. Only love, and kindness—the kind that's available through a parent alone.

"No, but—"

"So, you didn't give him the chance to tell you how he felt. You got scared and ended it before he could." My dad explains, and my head dips.

Mom glares at Dad, but he shrugs, taking another sip of his beer. She gathers me closer, and her arms feel more defined than last time. Something I note because there was a time when my mom was nothing but skin and bones from how sick she was. That tiny hint that she's healthy comforts me as much as the hug.

"Of course, she reacted that way. It's no wonder she's scared. A boy, well man, comes in wielding his entitlement like a sword, steals her little heart like he's her white knight, and then she realizes he's the villain instead."

"He's not a villain, mom. This isn't a fantasy."

"Got that right," Dad snorts from the chair. He finishes off his drink, setting the bottle on the floor.

If this were a fantasy, Nash would have swept me off my feet and pronounced his love to all of base camp. Instead of riding off in a stalemate, we would have been riding off toward happily ever after. He would be able to work from wherever, maintain his charming lifestyle while I bettered my village. We would have moved into my cottage, and he would have made it like his castle, and we would have adopted a tiny dragon to raise as our own. Despite my parent's best intentions, I was losing it.

My life, Nash's life, our lives were certainly not a fantasy.

CHAPTER THIRTY

NASH

"Are you dumb, boy? Or just plain stupid?" His finger digs into my chest.

Knew this was coming. I broke our deal, after all. When I asked Joe where I could find Hunter's fishing hole that morning, he laid out a list of demands, starting with, "You'll owe me some back straps," and ending with, "Don't you go fallin' in love with her unless you really mean it. And if you do, you better marry her." He said something about how Hunter was too good for the likes of me, too. It wasn't until I drove out of Blacktail Creek that I agreed wholeheartedly.

Joe looks out of place in my corner office. He wears a wife-beater tucked into old-school camo pants with more pockets than he knows what to do with. I'm in a suit that literally came from the shop today. His greasy salt-n-pepper hair peeks out of a backward cap, while my hair is freshly washed, if a little overgrown. I maintain three inches of height on his, and yet, I feel looked down on.

Moving out from under his finger, I find a seat behind my desk and motion toward the chairs across from me. The plexiglass chairs were almost never used since I met clients in the conference room, and my assistant never sat.

"I've got your elk at my place. I planned to have it delivered."

My chairs continue to go unused as Joe slams his fists on my desk, leaning toward me with a tight jaw. Should I be intimidated? Joe seemed like the type with a checkered past, and here he stood in my office without a single witness around.

"You know good and well this ain't about some back straps, City Boy."

"Sir, yes, sir," I taunt with a two-finger salute. Joe's face goes a bit red, but I pay him no mind. I'm going to need a drink for this. Pulling a bottle of whiskey from my bottom drawer, I set it on the table. Two glasses come next.

Guilt eats me alive. Up until this point, I never opened the bottle. My father gave it to me as a gift for making partner, made a joke about Don Draper when I stuffed it in my desk drawer. I always thought I'd open it when I closed my first major deal. Now, despite closing my biggest deal to date, I'm opening it over a woman.

Not just any woman. Hunter. All day, my view of the sky haunted me like the stacks of gear in my living room and the ache of my uncomfortable dress shoes. Never thought I'd wish for hiking boots, but here we are.

"You want a glass?" I ask, popping the seal. When I look back at Joe, he looks haunted. His eyes are on mine, but they look through me. "Joe?"

"Alcohol ain't gonna fix your troubles, kid. Mine neither," His words are tight when he whispers, "Put it away."

I pause what I'm doing, looking at the bottle. Still raw over losing Hunter; maybe it's not the best idea. I don't tuck it back into the drawer. Letting the bottle rest on the desk, I fold my hands in my lap, leaning back in my chair. Joe finally drags over one of my chairs, sitting on the ledge of it with his elbows resting on my desk. His eyes trail over the bottle before bouncing back to me. He says nothing, and I'm reminded that 'Intimidation Mode' means nothing to this man.

"If it's not about the back straps, tell me what you're really here for."

"Why'd Hunter come home cryin'?"

My heart stops in my chest. In all our time together on the mountain, I only ever saw her cry when she couldn't contain her anger. I left her in Blacktail Creek plenty mad, but from the way my heart stalls, I know he's not talking about rageful tears.

"She was crying?"

"You think I'd come down here to harass you like this if she wasn't? What'd you do?" His hand slams against the desk, and I sit forward, refusing to cower.

"Nothing! She broke it off with me," I argue.

Since my partner filled my schedule for my first day back, I didn't have time to build myself a defense on this. From the day in that trailer when Joe and I made the deal, I wondered how it would play out. Would I really fall in love with her like everyone thought? Even Jack Collister warned me off her, and I thought him crazy.

Hunter was a loud-mouthed, unapologetic, redneck woman from the moment I laid my eyes on her, plastering on a fake mustache.

Then, Hunter convinced me to sleep under the stars, trusted me to socialize for the both of us and tended to me when I was sick. This conversation with Joe became unavoidable because my feelings developed like wildfire. Slow at first before morphing into an out-of-control inferno. When she kissed me, riding the high of my first successful hunt, I never wanted the moment to end. Hell, when she stage-kissed me, I was like a dog with a bone hoping for a real kiss. Her lips on mine were a catalyst. Thoughts of the future we *could* have enveloped my mind.

"Nuh-uh. My Hunter wouldn't do that. You had to have said somethin' dumb."

"I told her I liked her. I planned to—"

"Liked her? That girl ain't at home cryin' about some slimy city-slicker that *liked* her. If you can't admit it to me, how're you ever gonna admit it to her?"

In no universe would I tell Joe that I loved Hunter before telling Hunter that I loved Hunter. So, I explain myself.

"She broke up with me," I whisper.

"She's scared." Joe groans, mumbling, "I gotta explain everything 'round here.

"That dumbass, Sam, broke her heart. Strung her along like a ball of yarn, weaving her into his life like it was forever. She didn't ask him for a thing, didn't mind his wild lifestyle, and would have followed him anywhere he went. All she wanted was a ring. The idiot couldn't even give her that."

Hunter had been vague about their entire relationship. She promised me she didn't care for him like that anymore, but she clung to my side like she needed my support. I didn't question her. Hunter knew her mind, and she would tell me when she was ready.

All I knew for certain was she deserved better than him.

"She thinks I'm exactly like him. She thinks I'm nothing but my money."

"I know damn well that ain't what she said."

"She's been calling me Bones since we met!"

What I wouldn't give to hear her calling me Bones right now.

Joe's bushy eyebrow raises, and I take a deep breath. I'll lower my tone. I repeat myself much softer. Joe only shrugs.

"And she calls me *ye olde fart* every once in a while. Do you see me stinkin'?"

"It's too late. I already messed up your demands. Do your worst and leave me to lick my wounds."

"You might not think you deserve her, Nash, but only you choose who you get to be."

Joe sighs, standing from the chair. Before I can protest, he snatches the bottle of whiskey and heads toward the door. A dull ache starts behind my eyes.

My head sinks into my hands. I made Hunter *cry*. How would I ever forgive myself?

When I don't hear the door close, I look at my visitor. The bottle hangs limply at his side, but Joe's staring at me.

"You have more to say to me?" I sound weak.

Not sure what piece of me wishes Joe will say something hopeful, some key to overcoming all the things in our way. That tiny seed of hope liquefies when Joe shakes his head with disappointment.

"If you don't go after her, you'll regret it 'til the day ya die."

CHAPTER THIRTY-ONE

HUNTER

The next morning, Mom makes pancakes shaped like Mickey Mouse, and Archer twirls through the door in a dress fit for a summer wedding. Layers of baby pink tulle flare out like a cloud around her hips, and a crisp white bow holds back elegant blonde curls. She floats in like a fairy before striking out for a hot pancake with no remorse. With one hand, she folds it into a single bite on the way to her mouth before shoving it inside.

"Uhhd mohnin," she greets.

"Don't talk with your mouth full," mom admonishes. Dad doesn't look up from this year's edition of hunting season's rules. He simply sips orange juice and crunches on his bacon.

Archer swallows down the pancake with an audible gulp before stealing my orange juice to rinse and repeat.

"Can I help you?" I turn toward the young menace and take in how truly similar we are. My Irish Twin, Archer, and I share the same long blonde hair and mom's blue eyes. In fact, all three of us kids have the eyes, despite Dad's eyes being a chocolaty brown. However, Fischer's built more like our dad, with a blockier nose and thinner lips. If it weren't for Archer's high cheekbones and skinnier face, you might think we were true twins. Especially when I keep my hair as long as hers.

Archer's arms come around my head, squeezing me against her chest until I'm shoving myself out of them and gasping for breath. "I'm so happy you're alright."

My brows pinch together, and my lips turn downward as I turn back to my food. I bring a protective arm up over my plate as Mom refills my orange juice glass. "Why wouldn't I be?"

"Mom said you'd been in a terrible accident."

"Mom!" I protest, she simply shrugs.

"It got her here, did it not?"

Archer didn't love Blacktail Creek like I did. She adapted quite well to their move to Arizona when she realized what a strip mall looked like and that she could see movies in real theaters. It didn't hurt that the population was a hundred times that of Blacktail Creek, and she could make friends her own age instead of following me around like a lost puppy. Archer attended college for Fashion Merchandizing and never looked back. She was no longer my aimless little sister. Archer knew who she was and where she belonged, and it wasn't her childhood home.

"I'm really fine," I grumble.

Her brows wrinkle like mine, and Mom scoots a plate over to her. There's a chip on the corner of it, but when it comes to food, nothing would stop a Hardy. "Mom said you had a run in with a bear, that your heart stopped."

My mouth drops as my eyes move from my sister to my mother. Momma Hardy shamelessly hums over the stove. Nary a blush of embarrassment in sight. When I look to Dad for backup, he doesn't even glance up from his magazine.

"There was no bear, and my heart is fine."

I don't even hear Fischer enter, but he lays a fat kiss on the top of my head with a "Glad to hear it, sis. I'm assuming Sucky Sam remains alive as well?"

"Mom, what did you tell them?"

My mother ignores me, but my siblings answer in sync.

"That we were celebrating Sucky Sam's demise over pancakes."

"That you were attacked by a bear so badly it stopped your heart."

My mother whistles Sweet Home Alabama and flips a heart-shaped pancake.

"Well, I wasn't attacked by a bear. My heart still beats, and Sam remains alive and well. Sorry to burst your bubbles."

"So, no bear?" Archer confirms.

"No bear," I agree before pinching my lips together tightly, "Well, one bear."

My sister's eyes brighten, "One bear?" She repeats.

"Maybe two."

"Two bears," My brother nods, stacking his own plate high with eggs and bacon. Definitely my father's son.

"Now, this I have to hear."

So, I tell the story again over pancakes, answering their peppering of questions as they came. In the end, I ended up back at the beginning to give context to how I knew Nash, and in the end, my sister squealed and clapped her hands.

"That's so romantic," she shoves my shoulder, "He saved you from *a bear!*"

"Two bears," Fischer teases.

"Two bears!" When her giggles die down, she looks around the front room. "So, where is this handsome knight then?"

"Well, that's why I actually called, darling." Mom pours me another orange juice as she explains that the handsome man who saved me from bears was why my heart was broken. I stayed quiet as she dramatized it for my sister, but Fischer's eyes stayed glued to me.

'You okay?' He mouths, and I give him a slight nod. Fischer wasn't the type to push me. So, if I said I was okay, he took that at face value.

Only this time, I wasn't sure it was the truth. Even surrounded by my family, tummy full of fluffy pancakes and fresh-squeezed orange juice, I didn't feel okay. My heart ached, and my mind told me I was stupid to get attached. The past weeks left me wrung out like a wet paper towel. I felt hollow, drowning in some places, starched in others.

I'll be fine.

"It's nice to have my kids all in one place," My mom hums, kissing my brother on the head.

"And it's the perfect opportunity to clean up the shop like we used to," Dad adds from the table.

Like a symphony, all of us siblings groan together.

My family stays for a week that we end with a traditional Hardy family Halloween. By which, I mean, three entire weeks early dad invites all his old buddies over for a barbecue.

Joe dresses up like a GI Joe. Mack and his wife Nicole wear their ratty Salt and Pepper costumes, and Dad embraces his figure with an 'Organ Donor' t-shirt that still makes us cringe. Mom wears fairy wings.

Miss Mabel brings the ambrosia salad and enough candy to cause a sugar crash in one hundred children. Mom cuts burger toppings into the shape of skulls. Archer dresses both Fischer and I, and we sing 'This is Halloween' about a dozen times despite it not being Halloween.

The chaotic flurry of it is the best part. No way to think about men from the city when I'm too busy snorting a pixie stick with my sister while my brother throws back a tube of sour spray like a tequila shot. We save our chocolate skulls and peanut butter pumpkins for later when the horror movie marathon begins. Inevitably, Archer falls asleep, leaving Fischer and I to watch alone until we grow bored.

My family leaves the next morning, a mess of hugs and tears from my mom. She just *loves it* when we're all together like this and demands that we all come to Arizona for Christmas. Dad gives us each a gruff but loving, "Proud of you, kid." He pairs it with a half hug, where he squeezes us into his side. We know he makes a point of it because his dad never said the same to him. Archer kisses both of my cheeks like we're the French and I'm not from Blacktail Creek. Fischer pulls us both under his arms in a headlock until Archer screeches about her hair. Then, he turns his attention to me and I wrestle him until we're both laughing.

They disappear in an instant, and because my mom refuses to be a bad guest, the house looks like they never came to visit at all. As the loneliness washes over me, it feels that way too.

CHAPTER THIRTY-TWO

NASH

My father called me first thing this morning.

"Son, I heard through the grapevine you haven't signed your deal with The Collisters."

Whoops.

After Joe came to visit, I closed my computer and went home. I dealt with the piles in my living room and deep-cleaned the scent of pine and wood smoke straight out of my apartment. The next morning, I called a specific style of delivery company to take all the elk out of my freezer and deliver it to Blacktail Creek. Then, I shaved my beard myself and drove straight to work before the sun ever even came up.

I had completely forgotten about it, or maybe I didn't want to go near anything with Hunter near it. How could I think about The Collister deal without thinking about her? Hunter had been integral to my achievement. It might be easier if she cashed her check. But she didn't, and I checked diligently.

"I've had my lawyers looking at it," I lie. Forgetting something as massive as a multi-billion dollar deal would leave me diminished in my father's eyes.

The week passed in a blur. Researching clients, preparing presentations, and presenting the packages to potential clients of Holden, Bushwick, and Carter Financial Firm. All while ignoring the urge to pack my stuff, quit my job, and show up on Hunter's doorstep like a stray dog. Numbers, stats, pep talks in the bathroom about how my face, as always, was handsome and deserving of this next account.

"That's interesting," My father says, and I know I'm caught. "Because my lawyers are your lawyers, and they've been chomping at the bit to get their hands on it."

"You know I'm going to accept it regardless of what they say. The early negotiations were clear. No, back and forth. Jack wanted it clear-cut."

The sun wasn't even up yet as I rode the glass elevator up to the top floor. All the partners had a corner office here, with a conference room at the far corner for the board.

"You refer to your client by his first name?"

"After months of hunting in the woods with him, I think I've earned it," I snap. Holding my phone away from my ear, I take a deep breath.

The elevator doors open with a soft chime, and I step onto the main floor. Past the reception desk, I head toward my office. My assistant holds out a small to-go cup without glancing up. Downing my coffee in one iron-hot gulp, I feel the burn in my chest as I enter my office.

I don't apologize to my father, instead I bring the phone back to my ear. He's speechless. I would be too if he spoke to me that way.

"Listen, The Collister account isn't typical by any stretch of the imagination. I know what I'm doing with it, and I would have expected you to understand that."

"Of course, I understand," He blusters, but I can tell he's backpedaling. He sighs and I prepare for a lecture.

The light in my office flickers on as I step into it, and I start up my computer before settling in.

"Son, I only want what's best for you."

We've had this conversation a hundred times. Whenever Mom sets me up with some new heiress—we want what's best for you. When I sealed a deal, I wanted to celebrate, but Dad was already speaking about the next one—want what's best for you. The sheer ignorance of my misery with every extra thing they put on my plate—what's best for you. Carter's always got the best. It didn't matter if it was the best for me or not.

Putting my father on speakerphone, I ignore my urge to sigh at his words.

"I'm opening it now."

I read it out loud to him. Lane opened it with some hopes of finding me well, and congratulations on securing the deal. He's CC'ed Jack and his wife, given me a return-by date that's swiftly approaching, and attached the document containing my future.

"Well, open the contract, Son."

I click the document, watching it download and open. My heart beats like hummingbird wings. Then, it's there.

My dad stays on the phone with me as I work through the entire contract. Most of it is standard agreements, outlines of the cash I'll be managing, point of contact information between legal firms, and the length of the agreement, with information regarding the extension of such. Then, the weird stuff starts popping up.

"Annual Hunting Obligation," I read off, skimming the paragraphs beneath.

"What?"

"Attendance at base camp will be required at the beginning of every archery season for a minimum allotted time of one work week."

"For what purpose?"

I skim some more, a smile tilting my lips, "Client relations."

Before my dad could get too up in arms, I read further, and a laugh burst from my chest.

"This isn't funny," My dad argues, "This is billions of dollars."

"Rights to Financial Advisor," I read out loud, "This agreement is entered into with the financial advisor, Mr. Nash Carter. If an advisor were to terminate employment, or employer to terminate employee, Collister and Co. would fall to Mr. Nash Carter's care. For an agreement to be made, this addendum must supersede any non-disclosure agreements.

"There are initial locations for every member of the board," I croak.

"Are you telling me that The Collisters belong to you? Not your firm?"

"With the majority of the board in agreement."

"Or they walk." I can hear the fear in my dad's voice. Money has never been a struggle, but losing and failing are two things he can't accept.

Luckily, I win either way.

"Or I walk, Dad."

We're both quiet for a long time. I stare at the end of the document. My dad takes in everything I've told him.

"I think you need to call your client, Son."

"What? Why?" I scroll from the top to the bottom, reading headers and cataloging what I might have missed.

"That addendum is a recipe for disaster. They need to take it out."

"The Collisters said they wouldn't do renegotiations. They don't want months and months of drafting."

"The board will never agree to it," He grumbles, and I can hear it. As part of the board, he'd never agree to it. Agreeing to it would give me the power to walk away with their biggest client, and despite my name being on the building, the board wouldn't trust me.

"The board has to agree to it. Otherwise the contract is null and void." Not quite true. I would sign this today, I would sign myself away to The Collisters for the remainder of their wealthy lives.

"Call your client. Talk him out of this."

Then, my dad ends the call.

I flip my phone over so it's face down on the table. Then, I read the contract again and again. With each pass over those special words, a plan forms in my mind. My dad would be proud because I did call my client, but he'd also be disappointed because I used that call to write a brand-new future.

CHAPTER THIRTY-THREE

HUNTER

The first Sunday of November rolls around quicker than expected. Snow blankets the ground, thick enough for me to pull out my proper boots. I'd already put up my dirt bike for the winter and weighted down the bed of the truck with some sandbags, but Hunter's Hardware needed to be winterized. So, despite my normal Sunday plans, I headed to work.

Monotonously driving from home to the shop allowed me too much time to think. As the weeks went on, and no word came from Nash, I started to believe everything between us really wasn't as serious as I first believed. Yet, the truck crunched over the fresh snow and ice and down the hill, and I thought about him, anyway.

With all the white, I didn't compare the trees to his eyes as much. The landscape looked different than it had during hunting season, and that made it easier. With the frost, I felt comfort for my cold heart.

I passed by Joe's house. The snow pushed up the loose board on his front step, and he'd pulled down the shutters for the winter. I wouldn't see a warm glow in there until spring when he opened them back up again. At least nothing changed between Joe and me.

Soon enough, the old lot was in my sights, except the pallet was gone. Glancing in the rearview, I see Joe's house, but when I look through my windshield again, the pallet sign is gone. There's no way anyone bought it. The lot practically returned to the wild. That sign had been there since I learned to bait my own line. Slowing my truck, I drive close to the shoulder, peeking around the trees carefully. As the vehicle comes around the corner, I see it.

A shed-looking shop like my own sits where the remnants of an old lean-to used to be. It's freshly painted with a thin layer of snow on its roof. There's a glass door on the front, and as my truck pulls closer, the shop name becomes visible.

Carter Financial Services.

My truck slides to a stop, slipping slightly in the snow. *There's no way.*

I look for some sleek black car or a hoity-toity head of well-groomed hair, but all I see is a neon open sign in the window and a sparkly blue truck parked by the tiny porch. My body moves before I order it to.

The truck door slams closed with a loud *bang*. My boots crunch across the ground. There's a proper path through the snow, and he's salted the two wooden steps. As I grab for the door, Nash stands on the other side, reaching for the door handle.

His eyes widen at the sight of me, and he glances over his shoulder. *That's right, buddy. No one's coming to save you now.*

Since he doesn't open the door, I do. I pull the handle, ripping it from his hand. As I'm about to ask him what he's doing here, he beats me to it.

"You're not supposed to be here."

I scoff, stepping back, and he steps through the door toward me.

"I'm not? I live here. *You're* the one who shouldn't be here."

"No, no. That's not what I mean. I meant—"

"Meant what? That I'm not supposed to notice my new neighbor? Was breaking my heart not enough? You plan to crush my business, too?"

He's shaking his head. His arms reach toward me like I'm a rabid dog instead of his ex-fake-girlfriend. Those haunting green eyes plead with me to let him off easy. Maybe he never knew me at all.

"That you're not supposed to be here today! I meant you're not supposed to be here today because it's Sunday, and you fish on Sundays."

My arms come across my chest, blocking him out the best I can. "The shop needed to be winterized."

He looks over at Hunter's Hardware and we can both see the drifts of snow piling in front of it. Frost tinges the windows, and it looks dreary inside. Located beside his new place, mine could use a fresh coat of paint. Good thing I had ten thousand of his hard-earned dollars waiting for a petty paint job. As soon as I think it, I know it's not true. It's too bad I'm morally pure. I'd never cash the dang thing.

As he searched my shop for all its many flaws, I searched him for the same. He remained the same. Bright eyes, dark hair, a baby pink polo shirt, and chinos that looked ridiculously out of place here. He didn't even have a coat on, and he'd been heading outside.

"What are you doing here, Nash?"

He opens his mouth to answer the question when a beautiful brunette slips out of the door, calling, "Who is this beautiful bombshell, Nish-Nash?"

She bumps him with her arm, looking up at him with interest, and that's all I have to see before I high-tail it back to my truck.

CHAPTER THIRTY-FOUR

NASH

Damn it. *Izzy has the worst timing.* I run after Hunter, completely overlooking the hazards of snow and ice as I slip and slide in my loafers. Winter clothes and shoes were on my list, but Hunter was my priority.

"Hunter, wait," I called, hoping she'd listen. Her truck door slammed closed, and she flipped me the bird.

When I called my dad to tell him I'd be leaving the firm and starting my own, he cursed me to high heaven. *'You're making a huge mistake, son.'* Still echoed in my ears. For about ten seconds, I thought about crying, and then I remembered why I did it.

Jack, Lane, and I all devised a plan. I would win Hunter back; I would represent the country men's finances, and everything would work out.

"Hunter, please?" I beg, reaching for her truck handle. She doesn't hesitate to pull her truck away. I hop out of the way to avoid her tire as she pulls back onto the road toward her house.

"Wait. That was Hunter?" Izzy asks, with her terrible timing once again. "She's way out of your league, bro."

Minutes after my dad hung up on me, Izzy showed up on my screen. She wanted to video call.

My sister was all bubbles and joy. I'd finally pissed off Dad, and she danced on my golden-boy grave. She announced, 'We can be proper siblings now!' and proceeded to explain that she would fly out to meet me at my penthouse.

At first, I didn't want her there. Her chaotic energy didn't help as I tried to piece together how I'd win Hunter over. I had a plan to get into her life, but I didn't know about after. That's when Izzy came alive.

She'd been sick of my sulking and demanded to know what was wrong with me. 'This can't all be about dad,' she said. So, I spilled my guts, ripped open my chest the way Hunter did, and told the whole sordid tale. My sister, smart as a whip, blamed me for it all. Then, she introduced the idea of a grand gesture.

Now, I'd completely screwed Operation Hunter before it even began.

Izzy bounds down the stairs, her arm coming around me. "For me, on the other hand," She waggles her brows, "I've got the best of both worlds. I look kind of like you, but I'm a girl."

"You're here to help me win her back, remember?"

"You're doing a great job."

"The sarcasm is unappreciated."

Hunter's truck disappears around the corner, and I contemplate the merits of following her in my own. As if Izzy can see my gears turning, she starts shaking her head.

"No, nope. Nuh-uh. That's not the move, big bro." She tugs on my arm, dragging me back toward the door of my newest office. Inside, the warmth of a space heater makes the place a drafty seventy degrees.

"I've got to go after her. No one's ever done that."

"No. You're going to sit, you're going to eat, and we're going to recoup some of your losses."

Izzy shoves me into my chair, shoving a pair of disposable chopsticks into my hand. She slurps her noodles easily while I push mine around the bowl of broth. I'm itching to go after her, drive until I find her truck, but whenever I try to stand, Izzy shakes her head.

"She'll come back, Nash."

"She won't."

"Her shop is right there. She has to."

A new idea floats through my mind. My sister is right. Hunter would come back, and when she did, we'd be ready.

CHAPTER THIRTY-FIVE

HUNTER

I'm not a runner. That's what I repeat to myself over and over again even as I drive the truck home, park it in the driveway, go inside for a nice cup of hot chocolate, and work up the nerve to go back to my shop. Blacktail Creek is my town. It's my sanctuary away from the Brads and the Chads and the Bones.

"Ugh!" I groan, planting my forehead on the butcher block counter. "I'm not a runner."

I stand from my chair and fight the urge to fall back into it.

"Buck up! Dang it." I screech at myself.

He looked so good, so right. Nash stuck out like a sore thumb in all this snow, but he built a cute little shop. Right next to mine.

But the girl. Who the hell was that girl?

I pace between the door and couch, repeatedly bending over to put on my boots but always backing out.

If I went back now, I'd have to see him again. Worse, I'd have to see the girl. The beautiful brunette with the eyes like autumn leaves and a floaty countenance like Archer's.

My feet halt in front of the mirror by the front door, and I force myself to meet my own eyes.

"You can do this," I growl. "You are over him."

I'm not. Not even a little over him, but the words give me strength to put my boots on again. I take the same monotonous drive, and instead of getting melancholy, I get angry. For months, he's been gone. No word. No nothing. Then, he shows up, buys the property right next to mine, and thinks what? That we can be friends? He's crazy.

Or maybe you're crazy. My mind taunts. She's a sore loser who wants to think he's here for me. But if that were the case, why bring the girl?

As my truck rounds the corner toward the shops, my jaw drops open on a gasp.

The snow around Hunter's Hardware has been plowed away and piled off to the side of my lot. Whoever did it—I have a clue—shoveled the concrete steps and laid down salt, too. As I pull into my spot and hop out, I see that more has been done. As I approach the door, I see colorful window displays for the holidays have been drawn on. One says, 'Ice-fishing? Get your bait here' and it's paired with a beautiful cartoon drawing in bright colored window paints.

Unlocking the front door, I head inside, and what do I see except a half-dozen little worker bees?

"Izzy, that's not a toy," Joe grumps, pulling the bow from the pretty brunette's hands. She rolls her eyes but places it back on the shelf where she found it.

Miss Mabel is here too. She has a handful of notecards decorated in the same pretty font as the window, and she's popping them in front of various items.

Nash is at the center. Instead of towering over everyone, making demands like usual, he's bent over the counter rubbing at a particularly stubborn scuff. A space heater I definitely didn't purchase warms the space from the back corner.

The door closes behind me, the tinkling of the bells announcing my arrival. All eyes turn toward me.

"Hunter," He whispers, and I freeze on the spot.

Buck up. You got this.

"Nash."

He bypasses the opening at the edge of the counter and hops over the top of it instead. Before he can reach me, the pretty brunette slinks between us with an outstretched hand.

"You must be Hunter. I'm Izzy. Nash's sister."

A laugh builds in my chest, bursting out right in her face. I slap away her hand, doubling over with my laughter. That's why she looked so dang pretty. She's Carter blood. The interest I'd seen had been over me. A sister meeting a significant other, not a lover interested in their person.

When I look up, there are tears in my eyes. Relief and embarrassment mingle like single kids at prom after finding someone to dance with. Her arms are crossed over her chest, her brows furrowed, and she looks so much like Nash. I don't know how I didn't see it before.

Her mouth tilts down in a frown, and as I stand and offer my hand, she rolls her eyes and walks away. Nash steps into my eyeline, and I hear her tell the group it's time for them to disappear. The doors shut, and we hear them laughing as they crunch through the snow, probably heading right next door.

I glance around the store to avoid looking at him, but instead I see all he's done for me. The place is completely ready for winter. The windows aren't just decorated, but they're treated for the cold, the rugs from the closet have been pulled out and beaten clean before being laid down in the aisle to avoid mud. He bought me a space heater. Everywhere I look, I see him.

His hand comes to my chin, gently tilting me upward to look at him.

"I got The Collister account," He starts, but I already know. It's what he paid me for to ensure he would get it. He killed an elk. I close my eyes, but when I open them, he's still staring at me. "Hunter, I got the account. Not my firm, not my partners, *me*. Wherever I go, they come with me."

"Congratulations."

A bit of anger sticks in my side like a thorn. Is this all he wanted to tell me?

"Thanks," He whispers.

I try to bite it back, but I can't. It's just not like me.

"That all you got, Bones?"

One side of his mouth tips up, and all that ice around my heart melts.

"No. No. I've got plenty more."

"Spit it out then."

"Well, once I knew the deal was tied to me, I realized there was nothing holding me back from what I wanted."

"And what did you want?" I push. That stupid flutter of hope I'd felt time and time again since he'd been gone crops up again. I'd pull into work and see a truck coming around the bend, hoping he'd be inside it. Sitting down at my fishing hole, I'd listen for him crashing through the brush. Even at Sunday dinners with Joe, I kept expecting him to show up like the random packages of elk in my freezer.

"You and me. Together on or off the mountain. Happy, in Blacktail Creek."

That melting heart pops a bleeder as his thumb brushes my cheek. In the moment I remember Jack telling me about forgiveness, and I understood Jennifer better now than ever before. Nash would be easy to forgive because I loved him.

"So, you thought, I'll buy a shop and stick it right next to hers?"

"Mhm, and a ring for her finger so I know I'm hers."

Nash doesn't waste a second. Falling to his knee in front of me, he digs out a little black box. Popping it open, I can't help but gasp.

Right above a beautiful teardrop diamond ring is a circle of purple rubber. It's one of those special rings for people who are hard on their hands or need something safe for work, and it's proof that he knows me. Tears prick my eyes.

"Hunter, I loved you from the second you stuck a fake mustache under that tiny little nose, and I'll love you until you're old and wrinkled. So, what do you say, love? Will you wear my ring and make me the happiest, sappiest man on earth?"

Snatching the purple ring from the box, I slip it on my finger. My lips land on his, and if Bones can't tell that's the closest he'll get to a yes from me, then he's got a lifetime to figure it out.

EPILOGUE

HUNTER

ONE YEAR LATER

Cacophonous yips and barks fill the room as we walk past the heavy metal door. A pimpled teen with an unflattering neon orange shirt walks us into the kennels to show us around. Dogs of all different shapes and sizes rush to their cage doors to peek at us, and I peer up at Nash with my best pleading eyes.

"One, Hunter. We agreed on one dog."

"But there's so many without homes," I argue. Turning my attention to the volunteer, I ask the right questions and they start telling us all about how generous it is to provide a home for more than one. The volunteer even steers us toward two puppies who have never been apart.

They're not the same breed. One looks like a tiny fluff of sunshine-yellow fur, and the other has ears bigger than its body. They tussle, the fluff ball nipping the big ear of the other. When I look at Nash, he sighs deeply.

"Can I pet them?" I ask the volunteer.

He leads us out to a small patch of grass, leaving me there for a minute before returning with the two puppies. They hardly notice we're there at first, still bickering and playing like siblings. But when Nash crouches down and makes some kissy noises, they rush toward him, and I melt.

Every day, it seems like I find another reason to love him more than the last. He's thoughtful and meticulous. He's a talented cook and a sophisticated kisser. Nash is the complete package and more. Honestly, how is a girl supposed to survive?

His big hands scritch both pups behind their ears, and the puppies melt beneath his hands. He coos to them.

"Who's a handsome boy?" He whispers to the floppy-eared hound, switching his attention to the fluff, "And our pretty, pretty girl."

For our twenty allotted minutes, we play with both puppies. We learn floppy-ears, who we're calling Eeyore, likes tug of war. Winnie, on the other hand, would rather play chase. By the end of it, all four of us are worn out, ready to eat our weight in treats.

The volunteer joins us outside again, asking, "What did you think?"

Looking to Nash—he's the decisive one between us—I'm not sure how he'll choose. Sweet Winnie or Sleepy Eeyore. He doesn't look down at me, but I squeeze his hand. It's meant to be a reassurance that any choice he makes is a good one. Then, he makes the best one.

"We'll take them both."

"Yes!" I shout, startling the puppies, who wake in a haze. Winnie runs without thinking, and Eeyore grumbles before tucking his hand right over his eyes.

Nash beams at me, shaking his head with disbelief.

"Told you," I shout again, running across the tiny yard with Winnie hard on my heels. I whoop one last time before settling enough to ask, "Where do we sign the papers?"

NASH

That night, we curled up on the couch. Hunter insists she will teach them that it's a boundary when they're bigger, but we both know she's too much of a softie. I don't mind either way. I only hope she won't complain too much when they shove her off the couch later in their lives.

Hunter had all kinds of big ideas for the two of them. She wanted to teach Eeyore to hunt bears, something I really wished against. For Winnie, she imagined her to be more of a duck hunter. Since both of our dogs supposedly needed to hunt like we do.

"They're the cutest things, right?"

Starting down at her, I arch a brow. "Absolutely not."

She nudges me, pointing at the sleeping puppies in her lap. They're insanely adorable, but I plan to stand by my opinion that Hunter is cuter.

"I happen to think you're the cutest."

She rolls her eyes at me. "I'm fierce, and wild, and stunning. I'm not cute."

"Lies." I kiss her nose.

She sighs.

I lean closer, bringing my lips a mere breath away from hers, but Winnie rolls to her back, sticking her legs against my throat and stretching. I back away, and the puppy rolls from my giggling wife's lap. With two hands, I put both dogs on the ground and crawled over her.

"Did you like your wedding present?" I whisper, catching her lips with mine.

She smiles against my lips. "They're perfect, huh?" *

"Undoubtably."

THE END

ACKNOWLEDGEMENTS

FIRST OFF, THANK YOU TO THE READERS AND THOSE WHO PARTICIPATED ON SOCIAL MEDIA (@MADI.VALE ON IG), PRE-ORDERED YOUR COPY, AND OTHERWISE ROOTED FOR THE LIGHT SIDE.

NEXT, THANK YOU TO MY WRITING COMMUNITY, ESPECIALLY MY SPRINTING FRIENDS. WITHOUT YOU, THIS BOOK WOULD HAVE TAKEN FOREVER (FOR NO GOOD REASON). YOUR CONTINUED DEDICATION TO YOUR OWN CRAFT INSPIRES ME.

FINALLY, THANK YOU TO THE MADISON VALE PUBLISHING CREW. THANKS TO LIBBY FOR PUTTING UP WITH MY CONSTANT QUESTIONS. THANKS TO ELORA FOR REASSURING ME OVER AND OVER AGAIN. AND THANKS TO MY HUSBAND FOR CONTINUING TO SUPPORT MY INDIE AUTHOR JOURNEY.

MADISON VALE PUBLISHING IS AN INDEPENDENT PUBLISHING IMPRINT FOR MULTIPLE PENNAMES OF A SINGLE AUTHOR. MADISON ROACH TITLES ARE FOR ROMANCE READERS WHO LIKE A SWEETER STORY. THEY ARE LIGHT IN BOTH EXPLICIT MATERIAL AND THEMES, IF YOU ENJOYED HUNTER'S HARDWARE, YOU MAY ALSO ENJOY HOPELESSLY DEVOTED- MADISON ROACH'S DEBUT NOVEL ABOUT LUNA SKYR AND THE WACKY ADVENTURE THAT ENSUES WHEN SHE *ACCIDENTALLY* JOINS A CULT.

9 798988 343974